Annie's Journey:
Denmark to Zion

a novel

To Quinn,
Love from your
grandmother,
Harleen
&

Annie's Journey: Denmark to Zion

a novel

Harleen Gross

Book design by Judith DeVilliers

Cover Photo by author taken at Fort Bridger Wyoming

ISBN 9781791572853

Printed in the United States of America

To:
Sheila, Steve and Shawn
and my beautiful grandchildren,
Jordan
Jeremy
Quinn
Max
Mila
Benjamin

Acknowledgements

My gratitude to my friends and familyfor their assistance and encouragement.

A special thanks to Judith DeVilliers for believing this story should be told and helping me with the book design. Thanks to my good friend, Lorna Burnett, for editing despite a broken arm.

Thanks to my sister, Helen Furr, for listening to me talk about this book for years, and giving me boundless encouragement to complete the story.

*I*ntroduction

Long before family history became a popular pasttime embraced by thousands, I began a persistent research for my ancestors. I wanted to know where they lived and what stories they would tell; if they could. I wondered about their personality traits, and what trials they overcame? I found that many of my ancestors emigrated from Europe during a time of great religious awakening.

My fourth-great-grandmother, Annie, immigrated from Denmark. She came to America during the greatest westward migration in United States history.

Fortunately, I found a brief autobiography, written by Annie. Thousands of records are now made possible through the worldwide internet, and Annie's life was no exception. Her experiences were similar to hundreds of other emigrants, and yet so remarkable, that I made it my personal goal to write her story. Annie's strong character and faith is to be admired and remembered forever, as we look for great heroes to emulate in our own lives.

In doing my research, I was fortunate to stand on the very soil of Denmark, where Annie lived and began raising her family. I was blessed to live eighteen months on the Mississippi River, and to also trace her steps across the Midwest from Kansas City, Missouri, into the Utah Valley.

I spent time alone at her grave and I prayerfully sought guidance in sharing her life.

This book was written for my own family and for all the hundreds of Annie's descendants. To Jordan, Jeremy, Quinn, Max, Mila and Benjamin, my grandchildren, may you always remember and never ever forget the sacrifices made by many of your ancestors that affords you the life you enjoy today.

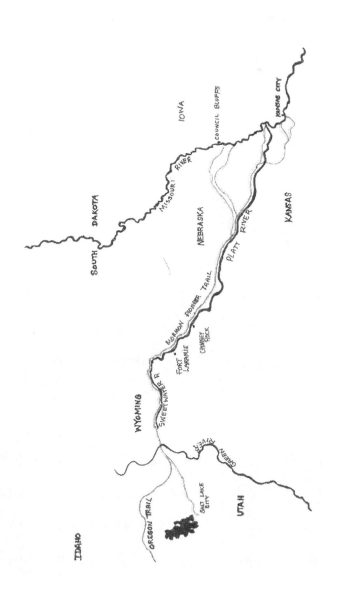

Contents

One

$\mathcal{A}$s a child, life seemed simple in Brejning. Our small Danish cottage was built close to the cobblestone street, the front door painted dark blue and the thick thatched roof was the insulation to keep us warm in the winter. Our family of seven included: father, mother, Hans, Catherine, Soren, Else and me. Else was five years old when I was born. When I was born, mother's hair was silvery grey, her back hunched over from years of hard work, and she had lost much of her energy for parenting.

Mother relied on Else's enthusiasm to tend me. Else learned to bath and feed me, and we played together while mother took care of other household chores. Mother did not stop to play with us; she was always working and her voice was strict and stern. We were all given individual responsibilities, and if we did not do what she said, we knew there would be serious consequences, no matter the reason. Mother was quick to quote the aged advice from Proverbs, "Idle hands are the Devil's workshop."

Else and I slept in the same bed, and when the winter winds blew and our breath danced around like fog, I would complain. "Else, I am cold. My toes are freezing."

"Annie, put your feet on mine, and I will warm your toes." I would snuggle my body against hers, and once my feet were warm I would drift off into a dreamland of fairies and fantasy.

Else and I were petite, but we made up for our size with abounding energy and curiosity. We went exploring in the golden fields of wheat, hiking up our skirts so we did not trip in the furrows. Else held my hand as we walked around the marsh, watching for wildlife. She told me about the field mice, and how their family lived in a hole deep in the dark soil. We walked along the water's edge of Vejle Fjord, looking for shells and splashing through the cool water. "If you watch, Annie, you might see the beautiful mermaids that live under the sea." I never saw a mermaid, but I believed. I dreamed of being a mermaid and exploring the depths of the sea. That would be magical.

One day in the spring, Else and I sat in the tall grass near our home. Our green eyes were glued to a huge nest anchored near the chimney of our thatched roof. Else explained. "The storks chose partners before they return from their winter feeding grounds, and now that spring has arrived, they come back to their old nest and lay their eggs."

"How many eggs do they lay, Else?"

"Last year we saw four babies, but we will not know for sure until they hatch. Fader says he is pleased to have the storks return because they bring happiness and good luck to our home."

We watched and waited for weeks. "One of the storks must always stay in the nest to keep their eggs warm." Else continued. "It takes almost a month for the eggs to hatch, but we will not see the babies for a long time."

I grew weary of waiting. However, early one summer morning the wait was over. "Else, hurry. Come look. The baby storks are out of their nest." Walking along the pitch of the thatched roof were four baby storks, awkwardly balancing on their gangly long red legs. I loved the storks. I wished I could fly.

Mother taught Else how to make bread, and I begged to help. I stood on a small homemade stool, and Else measured the flour. I measured the lard. We took turns stirring and mixing. We had to be careful because mother scolded us if we spilled the flour. "You girls are being too silly, and now look what you have done."

"Annie. Watch me. Knead the dough, back and forth until the dough is smooth and creamy. Do not hurry. Be patient because this part is important." Else let me pinch off small balls of dough and put them into a greased pan. Then I covered the pans with a cotton cloth while we waited for the dough to rise.

In the fall we made candles. It was a family affair. Candles were critical to our lives in Denmark, because of the long dark winters. When our animals were slaughtered, and the meat put away for the winter, mother cooked down the fat. "Annie. Watch me." Else would say. "Hold the wick like this and slowly lower it down into the fat. Be careful not to get burned on the pot."

Mother explained. "Remember that old woolen shawl that the mice ate a hole in? I saved the shawl just for this day. We are going to braid strands of the shawl to make wicks. Soren has tied a small pebble to one end of the wick for a weight, and on the other end he has tied a small stick."

"Watch me, Annie. Just hold the stick like this and dip it into the fat slowly. Now pull it out, let it drip just a minute, and then we will hang it over this rack to dry."

"And you only have to dip the wick in the fat, let it dry, and dip it again about thirty five times just to make one candle." Soren grumbled.

"Let me do it." I was anxious to try. "I am not a baby."

We were all exhausted at the end of the long process. It was a busy long day of dipping and drying and storing the candles in straw-filled boxes. Mother kept a small box of candles in a cool place inside the kitchen, but the rest were buried in a box to the back of the house. "If we do not bury the boxes of candles, those mice, the very ones that you think are so "cute," will have a feast, and our work will be wasted."

"How many candles do you think we made today?" Soren removed his boots by the door.

"I would say we have at least three hundred." Mother untied her apron and placed it over the back of a kitchen chair. "I can tell you, I am glad candle making is over for another year."

I learned to do most household chores including the laundry. It was a full day process of scrubbing, and backbreaking work for anyone, most especially a young person. I helped in our garden with the planting, watering, weeding, and harvesting of our produce. "I can not keep up with these terrible weeds." Mother complained. However, when she creamed the potatoes and peas together for supper, alongside a piece of pork roast, we all forgot the hours of work it took to make that meal possible.

At night, after the candles were blown out, and before we drifted into sleep, Else would tell me her secrets. She talked about love. "What is love?" I ask in innocence. Else's voice changed, and I could almost touch her excitement through the dark.

"Love is caring deeply for another person." Else responded. "I have a friend at school. His name is Jasper. After school, we hold hands when we walk home. We have even kissed each other."

"He kissed you?" I gasped at the thought.

"Yes, he kissed me on my cheek. It was wonderful. I thought my heart would stop." Else paused. "You are too young to understand. Someday you will learn about love. But for now, you are too young." Else whispered. "Annie, this is our secret. Do not dare tell Moder."

Else was beautiful. She kept her blonde hair pulled away from her face, and she had a smile that charmed most of the men in Brejning. She was brilliant and confident, impressing others with her knowledge and skills. Else finished her formal education when she was just sixteen. One day, I accidentally overheard Else and mother in a heated conversation. "What do you mean, Else? You can not stay here in Brejning and do nothing. There is no work for you here in this farming area."

"I do not care, Moder. I do not want to move to Vejle" Else's voice made the window coverings quiver. "You can not send me away like this."

"Else. Watch your tongue. Do not ever speak to me in such tones again. I know you do not want to move to the city, but it is time for you to contribute to the family income. It will be easy for you to find work in Vejle."

Mother sat two small cups on the table. "Sit down and have some tea, Else. I'm sure you will feel better with some of my peppermint tea." Else hesitated. Tears filled her eyes as mother continued. "Remember my friend, Sigred?"

Mother fussed with her apron. "Sigred has a friend in Vejle named Ms. Jensdatter. Ms. Jensdatter will give you a room until you find work."

I will always remember the day Else left home. Else gave me a peck on the cheek. "See you soon, Annie." Then she turned her head, so I could not see her tears, and walked away with a little leather case containing her belongings. I could barely breathe at the thought of Else not being near. She was my best friend, my teacher, my confidant, and oh, how I adored her.

Else did not come back to Brejning for several weeks, but when she did, it was not the same. Even though Else's world was just two hours away, it might as well have been another world. The emotional distance between us was even greater. "Tell me all about it, Else. I want you to tell me everything. Where are you working? Tell me about the city. What is it like?"

Else began. "I lived with Ms. Jensdatter just a few days. She knew someone that worked at The Manor, a beautiful mansion in Vejle, and I was hired to work as a housemaid. You should see this mansion, Annie. The rooms are filled with lavish trimmings and hand woven carpets from far away places. The walls are decorated with precious paintings, and the ceilings in the rooms are so high that it seems they reach the heavens.

"I have rarely seen the mansion owners. They are usually traveling to far away places. Once I saw the lady of the house. She was wearing a lavish long flowing gown. She looked like a queen, but I did not speak to her."

"The mansion sounds breathtaking. What is your room like, Else?" Mother inquired.

"Well, that is the hardest part, Moder. My room is in a very cramped and dark area of the attic, with just one small window for light. I have to share the little room with two other maids. I was told that come winter it will get very cold and damp in our room. It is sweltering right now."

Mother shook her head and mumbled under her breath. "What is a woman to do with such spoiled children?" Then mother flashed a sarcastic smile and went back to her mending. "You will be just fine Else. You will be just fine."

Else stopped coming home. She sent an occasional letter, to let us know how she was doing, and she sent money to mother. I missed Else terribly. Without Else's help at home, I could not always attend school. "I need you to stay home from school today." Mother begged. "I am not feeling well." Mother honestly struggled to do all the work at home and I struggled to do the right thing. How could I help her and also attend school?

I finally finished my formal education at the age of nineteen. I was anxious to find work and be on my own. I had no desire to move to Vejle, near Else. I needed to stay in Brejning and be able to help mother and father, as needed. I became the youngest of four house-workers employed by a wealthy elderly couple. I worked long hours. I was expected to be up early, and I often worked late into the evening, but my employers were polite and caring.

Now that Else and I were both employed, we rarely saw each other. However, one afternoon my co-worker, Catherine, found me in the kitchen. "Annie, there is a woman at the servant's entrance asking to see you. She says her name is Else."

The moment I stepped out the door Else grabbed me. She buried her head into my shoulder; her body limp and broken like a little child. She sobbed and gasped for breath, then finally whispered in my ear. "I have to talk to you, Annie. Where can we talk in private?"

"We can talk right here. There is no one else around, Else." I waited for her to begin.

Else stood tall, and took a deep breath. "I am in love, Annie, with a young man in Vejle. His name is Hans. He is a garden worker at the mansion. I tried to avoid him, because I knew if anyone discovered we were sneaking out together at night, we would both be discharged.

"At first I tried to tell him no. I told him that we could not continue to meet, but it seemed impossible. I dreamed of him. I longed to feel the touch of his lips on mine. Alas, we could not stay apart. Our attraction to one another was stronger than either one of us could ignore."

I held Else's hand, trying to console her. "Then what happened? Let me guess, your employer discovered you were meeting in secret?"

"Yes. Someone must have seen us together and told. But that is not the worst part, Annie." Else took a deep breath, and in between the sobs, she blurted the final phrase that changed everything. "Annie. I am going to have a baby."

I was speechless. It seemed like time stood still as I searched for the right words. This was not the strong-willed woman that I knew. Else was the one usually giving me advice, but this time was different. Else was depending on me.

"It is going to be okay, Else. We will find a way to work this out." I paused for just a brief second then I threw my arms around her. "I love you Else. We will work this out together." I ask the obvious, difficult question. "Have you told Hans about the baby?"

Else's sobs grew even louder with the thought. "No. I have not been able to talk to him. I could not find him before they escorted me off the property."

"Else, you must find Hans as soon as possible. Tell him. If he loves you, he will be there for you. Believe in love Else, remember! Remember you taught me about love when we were young."

I could see the strength and courage filling Else's eyes. "Yes. You are right. I need to find Hans and tell him. I am sure he is wondering what happened to me."

"Do you need me to go with you?"

"That is not necessary, Annie. Now that I am thinking more clearly, I think I know where I can find him." Else squeezed my hand, dried her face, and turned back towards Vejle. "Oh, and Annie. Do not breath a word of this to Moder."

Hans was there for Else. When she told him she was going to have his baby, he insisted they be married. He did not hesitate. "We will be married next month or next week. The first thing we need to do, however, is talk with the Reverend and apply to have the Banns read in church. Once that requirement is met we can be married properly. Do not worry, Else, we will find a little room in town to live and I will find a place to work with better pay."

Mother was there for Else, also. "I have the perfect solution." Mother smiled. "Will you please come live with your father and me? We are both getting old, and it is hard to keep up. You would be helping us a great deal."

The Reverend Johanson performed the marriage of Else and Hans in the Gauerslund Kirke on November 13,1828. We all fell in love with Hans. He was genuine and polite, and most of all, there was no doubting that he loved Else. Well, everyone loved Hans except father. It would take some time before father could forgive Hans for what he had done.

Indeed, having Else and Hans living with our parents was the perfect solution. I worried less about mother and father; and Else's life began settling down. It did not take too long for Hans to find work on a pig farm. My goodness, he was a hard worker. Else's firstborn came in January. Jens Peter was his name. It was about three weeks later when we all gathered together for the christening of Jens, in the Gauerslund Church.

Else was thrilled beyond imagination when she gave birth to her second child, a daughter. Else named her, Cecilane. Else was so happy. She loved to fuss over her family. She fussed over the little house. Else fussed over Hans. My goodness, she kept him happy with traditional Danish foods prepared from mother's recipes.

"Else, you are a wonderful wife, and you are an amazing mother. I can hardly wait for my days off work so that I can come to visit." Those years were wonderful. We were adults now, sharing a deeper kind of love and friendship.

Perhaps, someday I will find a love of my own.

Two

"When ends life's transient dream,
When death's cold sullen stream
Shall o'er me roll,
Blest Savior, then, in love,
Fear and distrust remove—
O bear me safe above,
A ransomed soul."
[Ray Palmer]

It seemed as though the whole community was at the Gauerslund Kirke the morning of February 9, 1835. A foot of snow could not deter father's friends and neighbors from paying their last respects. After all, father had lived his seventy-one years in Gauerslund Parish, and he knew almost all the villagers.

Gauerslund Kirke was the center of the Parish, both figuratively and literally. It was the place where all people worshiped according to the King. Every church of Denmark was declared to be the National Church of Denmark or Evangelical Lutheran. We were proud and humbled to worship in one of the most ancient churches of the country. Clergy of Gauerslund Kirke had performed and recorded the history of marriages at the altar of the kirke, infant baptisms at the font and funerals for the deceased for centuries.

Else and I sat on each side of our mother during the service. Our siblings and their children, our cousins and their families filled the first four rows of the chapel. My two uncles had long since passed, but their families were there. Father's only sister, Maren, sat with her children and grandchildren. Father's grandchildren now counted twenty-one! My brother, Hans, already had five of his own. His little ones were so cute, all huddled close to him and his wife. They were just precious. *I love to see our family together. Sad that we don't take time to gather except at a funeral. I wonder if I will ever have a family of my own.*

"Annie, hold on to mother's arm when we walk out, just in case. She is very frail."

"Moder, how are you feeling?"

"I am quite alright. Do not fuss about me, girls."

Voices of the congregants filled the nave. Never do I remember a hymn so comforting, and words so full of hope. Reverend Johanson's sermon, however, was way too long. The children were restless, and Aunt Maren was asleep. I was exhausted. Finally, the benediction was read and Reverend Johanson announced to the congregation. "Will the congregation please stay seated while the casket of Mads and his family exit to the narthex. The congregation will then be invited to extend their condolences to the family before they exit the kirke."

The clergy led the procession, with my brothers, Hans and Soren, helping to carry fathers casket into the narthex. Else and I walked with mother, holding her arms as we walked past the pews filled with friends. The pipe organ continued to play as the procession worked its way into the narthex.

"That was a beautiful tribute." Else whispered. Then, without any warning, mother launched into a high pitched prolonged mournful cry. I was so surprised, and I thought Moder might fall to the floor. I knew mother was full of grief, but I did not understand just how much until her grief took a voice. "Moder, I am going to get you a chair to sit on. Annie and I will stand next to father's casket so that we can greet our friends as they leave the kirke."

One friend after the other extended their condolences. "Your father was one of the hardest workers I ever knew. If there is something I can do for you, Sidsel, please let me know."

"Else, did you know that your parents were married the same day we were, forty-five years ago! So nice to see you again, Annie. Where are you working?"

"Annie, I would like you to meet a friend of our family." Else's husband, Hans, made the formal introduction. "Annie, this is Jens Jesperson. He is from Sellerup and knew your father for many years."

Extending my hand, I shook the hand of Mr. Jesperson. "So pleased to meet you. How kind of you to come." I responded. Jens was a tall, rather large man with dark brown hair and deep-set eyes. We spoke briefly, and Jens moved aside.

I was quite surprised when Jens Jesperson came calling on me the Sunday after father's service. I felt rather awkward, sort of like the red-legged baby storks on top of our family home. Why would Jens call on me?

The first day we just walked together, down the cobblestone streets of the village. We talked about our families. "Moder is going to be lost without fader. They have never been apart since they were married."

"My fader passed away about five years ago." Jens hesitated, his voice filled with emotion. "Fader's passing was hard
for me but much more difficult for Moder. She didn't think
she could go on without him. I think she eventually found
comfort by helping others and doing good. She seems to
keep busy these days."

"Do you help your moder with the animals, or whatever
she needs?"

"I did, but after fader passed we sold the milk cow. Moder could not take care of a garden, but she does have some
flowers she enjoys tending."

"My moder is really blessed to have Else's family living
with her. They will help her, and keep her busy."

Jens was industrious and hard working, a blacksmith by
trade. Unlike the majority of men in Denmark, he owned
his own small farm. Jens was always looking for ways to get
ahead financially, and because of this, he also owned and
operated a small business of brick making.

Both Jens and I worked every day except Sunday. Conse-
quently, we only saw each other one day a week. Without
fail, I could anticipate Jens walking the three miles from
Sellerup to Brejning just to see me. Sometimes we would
meet at Gauerslund Kirke and worship together. After
church services, we walked through the adjoining cemetery
filled with stone markers of friends and family. The cemetery was groomed with pebble paths, and planted with flowers of all kinds. Spring filled the paths with daffodils, crocus
and my favorite, tulips.

When summer came we walked along the grassy old

church dike, built of boulders several hundred years ago. We would find a place to sit and talk. I couldn't imagine how we could find so much to talk about, but we did. It was easy to be with Jens.

"Jens is a good man, Else. He is such a hard worker. He is very kind to me. I love that he has a tender heart. You know, he has never been married before. I know why, too. He is always working! I think he must work night and day."

"I think that has all changed now, Annie. Since Jens met you he has gone out of his way to court you, and to show his interest. You two have been keeping company for months."

"Else. Oh, Else. I wish it were that easy. I enjoy his company and he is courteous and kind to me. He has his own business and would be a good provider."

"Annie, look at what Jens has to offer you. He has property, a real farm, with a horse and a garden. You will have your own home. Jens told me he would build a house for you."

"It all sounds good, but you do not understand. Else, I don't *love* him. When Jens holds my hand, my heart does not get all excited. My heart is confused. I am happy being on my own. I am not sure I want to give that up."

"Love will come with time, Annie. Real love is not an emotion, but a choice. Love will come because of your choice." Else challenged me.

Jens knew I loved flowers, and he brought me bouquets of wild roses and daisies. One day Jens walked to Brejning to get me, and then we walked together back to Sellerup to explore Jens's farm.

"Come this way, Annie. This is my blacksmith shop. I was about fourteen when my parents sent me away for my apprenticeship. I studied about six years before becoming a journeyman."

"Why didn't your father just teach you the skills?"

"I guess that could have been an option, but he said he did not want me to learn his bad habits. Besides, I received food, lodging, and a basic education during those years. Then I came back home to work with Fader. Blacksmithing is dirty work, but it is worth it. I enjoy working with the iron. I heat the iron rods in the furnace, or forge, which softens the metal. That allows me to shape it by pounding the iron with a hammer on this anvil. The furnace burns most all day, and the bellows keep the fire hot. It takes a lot of skill to make simple utensils, like these, or farm tools, like this blade for plowing."

"What is this? A horseshoe?"

"Yes, it is, Annie. I make the iron shoes as a blacksmith, but I also trim and balance the hooves of equine, then place a shoe on their hooves, if necessary. That skill is known as a farrier."

Jens' work was much more technical than I had ever imagined. I was quite interested, but I kept thinking about my skirt dragging through the dust on the dirt floor. The odor burned my nose and my stomach felt queasy. "Come with me, Annie. Let us get out of here and go meet my mother. Mette Catherine is her name."

Meeting Mette was worth the whole trip. "Please come in, Annie. Jens has told me all about you. I hoped I would meet you soon." Mette brushed crumbs off the tablecloth and offered us a seat at the table. "How about a cup of coffee? I have some fresh pastry."

Mette was a short round little woman with dimples and frosty grey hair. She loved us being there. She hung on every word I uttered, and when Jens said it was time to go, Mette reminded him that we had not been there long enough. "Please come back soon, Annie. I will be looking forward to it."

But, I love where I work. I enjoy the home and the people I serve. Most of all I love the independence. All my life I was told what to do. I was told what to wear and where to go. I have been treated like a baby most of my life. Finally I have freedom.

I hesitated about a commitment to Jens. Could I give up all the comforts and freedom I now enjoyed? I continued to see Jens, every Sunday and by summer it seemed to me that Denmark was a little more colorful, the flowers more fragrant, and each Sunday my walks with Jens became more comfortable. I continued my personal debate, second guessing my decision. Could I tell Jens "yes" if he asks me to marry him?

Mother loved Jens. "Please come for dinner next Sunday. We love having you, Jens." If mother did not invite us, Else did. Else was fascinated with Jens. Jens was not shy and seemed to be knowledgeable of current activities in our community as well as the country. Jens would talk about the issues with government, the oppression from the monarchy, and the future of Denmark. Jens talked about our community and how the people must work together if we are to keep our small farms alive and survive on the land. Jens knew the Bible, and we talked about the Sunday sermon and how we could apply the message in our personal lives. "God is love." Jens would say. "We must love one another and most of all, be kind to one another. It is really quite that simple."

Dinner at mother's house on Sunday was routine. One Sunday Jens knocked at the door, and Else let us inside. Suddenly, with squealing and shouts of pure delight, Jens Peter, and Cecilane, Else's children, came running to greet me. "Aunt Annie! Yea! Aunt Annie is here!" They hugged my legs and their little green eyes looked into mine. Suddenly, the uncertainty I had about Jens disappeared. I had been touched by the hearts of love. Else's home was filled with innocence and laughter, wonder and love because of her children. I wanted to have a home like that.

Jens took my hand in his as the reverend read aloud from The Gospel of Mark. "But from the beginning of the creation, God made them male and female. For this cause shall a man leave his father and mother and cleave to his wife, and they twain shall be one flesh."

"Anne, do you take this man to be your lawfully wedded husband, to cherish, to obey, to love and to honor until death you do part?"

"I do." I responded, my voice barely audible.

"Jens, do you take this woman to be your lawfully wedded wife?"

"I do." Jens' voice was loud and clear, echoing among the pews.

Our families gathered together in the Gauerslund Kirke and witnessed Jens and I pledge to love and honor each other until death we would part. We became husband and wife before the Holy altar of God on August 1, 1835.

Have I ever second-guessed my decision to marry Jens, you ask? No! Not then, not ever.

Three

*B*efore we married I thought I had a clear understanding of how my life would change. "I will manage the blacksmith responsibilities, Annie. You will need to take care of the house, the animals, and the garden." I knew when we started a family I would also be in charge of the children, their well-being, and education. From the beginning, I knew I would be working much harder than I ever had, but I was committed to being Jen's partner.

It did not take long to realize I did not totally understand how many hours Jens actually worked each day. It seemed as though Jens never rested. I had also underestimated the significance of Jen's business to the community of Sellerup. It seemed that our blacksmith shop was the hub for every man and woman around town. It was the place where many business deals were made. It was the community news center and Jens would keep me informed.

"Annie, did you hear about the Petersen's? Their youngest child is gravely ill. Would you mind taking some soup over for the family? I forgot to tell you that Peter Neilson has ordered a new farm wagon. The money from that will certainly help our business. Oh, and I heard that Peter's daughter, Ester, is getting married."

Jens made and repaired tools for farming and household tasks, but he also fixed carts and wagons. Jens always said.

"A job well done is a job never seen again." That was not exactly true, however, because he had a considerable amount of repeat business with shoeing horses.

Jens had not received special training in these other professions, but it came out of necessity when friends ask him. "Jens, can you take a look at this?"

Our house was a one-room structure made of sod with one door and three small windows. The outside was covered with stucco and the inside had a wooden plank floor. We had a stove for heat in the winter, and the stucco insulated the house quite well. The roof was heavily thatched so that we did not worry about the winter rains or snow. However, I was not content with status quo.

I am going to make this house into a home. If I put the table over in the far corner I would have more room to work around the stove. I am going to decorate these barren walls and make needle binding covers for the table and drawers. I have some wool scraps. I will use them to make a quilt for the bed and rugs for the floor.

In the spring Jens turned the soil and I planted the garden. Jens surveyed my work. "Wonderful. The garden looks amazing, and the soil so rich, Annie. We should have a beautiful harvest this year."

"Did you notice the tea rose that I planted next to the house." I was very pleased with myself. Jens was too.

Not long after we married, Jens took our new wagon to fetch mother and Else for dinner. I was not sure that mother would feel up to the ride, but there she was. "Moder, I am so pleased that you came. How are you feeling?"

Mother smiled. "Annie, I could not feel better. Thanks to Jens for bringing us to your new home. I am so pleased to be here with you."

We embraced and exchanged pleasantries, all the while mother scrutinized our home. "Annie, I am so proud of you. It looks like you have added your own special touch. I love the hand work on your tablecloth."

Else also heaped a pile of generous compliments on me. "Annie, the dinner was excellent. Your roast was tender, and the potatoes were perfect. Your little home is quite comfortable and cozy. I am so proud of what you have done."

Else's third child was due to arrive about April of 1838. I tried to hide my disappointment. I was full of envy wishing it were me waiting for a baby to come. "Jens and I have been trying, Else. I do not understand why I have not been able to get pregnant."

"Not to worry, Annie. Your time will come. If you could get Jens away from his work for a few days, perhaps that would help." Else teased me.

It was mid-February, and we were still in the grip of winter. I was working on my quilt, enjoying the quiet, when Jens burst through the door. He stomped the snow off his feet, and without a word, removed his heavy coat, hanging it in its place by the door.

"What are you doing, Jens? My voice filled with frustration. "Are you feeling all right?"

He did not have to say anything. I could tell something was terribly wrong. His silence sent chills down my spine. "Annie. I do not know how to tell you. Hans sent word through friends who came to the blacksmith shop. I received the news just a few minutes ago."

"What are you saying, Jens? Is it Moder? What is wrong with Moder?"

"No, Annie. It is Else. Apparently, she went into labor during the night, and by the time Hans realized her condition was critical, it was too late. Hans sent for the doctor, but by the time the doctor arrived, Else and her premature baby could not be saved."

"No. No. This can not be so." I screamed. "Tell me this is not happening, Jens." He held me close, trying his best to somehow comfort and lessen the pain.

"We must go. We need to go to the house to be with Moder and the children. Please, Jens, hurry. Take me there."

The ride into Brejning seemed way too long. I rushed through the front door of the old home, still hoping to find things remaining the same. I envisioned seeing two little children, full of excitement because we were there. I imagined mother, busy in the kitchen, helping Else prepare a meal for guests.

"Thank God you are here, Annie." Hans stood from a chair and pulled me to his side. "Annie. I am so sorry." Tears soaked his face. "I tried to do everything. I could not do anything. I fetched the doctor, but by the time he got here, it was too late. Annie, she is gone. What am I going to do without her?"

"Oh, Hans. Tell me. Where is Moder? How is she doing?"

"Moder said she was not feeling well and went to her room."

"Moder, it's Annie. I am here." I wanted to put my arms around mother and hold her tight. I could not imagine the pain of losing a child, especially one as precious and young as Else.

Mother faced the wall, motionless. "Moder. I am here."

"She is gone, Annie. Else is gone. How can I go on living without Else?"

"Moder, do not talk like that. I am here, and I will take care of you. Hans and the children are here. We love you. We will take care of you."

The day was filled with family and friends calling at the house. They came calling with plates of food and condolences, hoping to ease our pain. We huddled together, our little family, and tried to make sense of it all.

"We need to get started back home, Annie. I will bring you back tomorrow if you would like."

I tried to sleep. All night I tried to sleep, but instead, my mind played a continuous melody of memories. Sleep was but a flicker. It was still dark when Jens arose and went to the blacksmith shop. "I will be gone a couple of hours. Be ready when I come back and we will go to your Moder's."

I had only begun cleaning the dishes when Jens stood in the doorway. "That was quick. I am not ready yet." His boots were covered with fresh snow. "Let me finish doing the dishes."

"Annie. Look at me. I need to tell you something. I had barely arrived at the shop when another messenger came from Brejning. It is your mother, Annie. Your Moder passed away during the night."

I think no one is ever prepared for the final breath of their parents. I know I was not. Jen's words seemed to echo over and over. "Your Moder has passed away." My knees began shaking and I collapsed. I felt the pain deep in my soul, and I was overcome with a long mournful wailing.

Eventually, everyone affected by the devastating loss of their wife, or their mother, their sister or their friend somehow adjusts. That is what you do when someone passes away. You make do. You just get through the dark days. You cling to the promise that "Sunday will always come."

I usually loved spring, but I barely noticed the flowers that year. I went through the motions as if I were lost. But then, I had just lost my mother and sister. Hans brought his children to visit frequently, but I could not seem to move on.

Hans hired help to care for his children, and soon his grief found consolation with another woman. I think Else would have been disappointed that Hans did not wait for the usual year before he moved on with his life. He did not even wait six months! I did not dare repeat what the townspeople were saying. "Why, Else would turn over in her grave if she knew Hans was already married."

"Jens, I do not understand why I am feeling so ill. I just want to sleep all day."

"Perhaps you should talk with my Moder. She would love to help you."

I described my depression to Mette. She was good at listening. "I am feeling sick when I get up in the mornings.

I just go back to bed and sleep half the day away. I do not know how to shake this depression, Mette."

"Is it possible that you are with child? After all, you told me that you two have been trying for some time now."

"With child? No. I do not think so." The thought had never occurred to me. "You really think so, Mette?"

Once I had my pregnancy confirmed, each new day became more joyous. I was convinced that the gift of my own child was the healing gift, given by the mighty hand of the God that cared for us all. I thought I could hear Else whispering again. "The Lord giveth and the Lord taketh. Blessed be the name of the Lord."

I found joy in my steps again. When I needed someone to talk with, Mette was there. She was my angel. She was my mentor. "I brought dinner for you two. I hope you enjoy the fresh bread I baked this afternoon."

"What would I do without you Mette? I would be lost, for sure."

Our first child was born in November. Mette was there with the midwife, thrilled to be a part of the miracle of birth. Jens went to the blacksmith shop. He could not stand to wait and not be able to do something to help. Mette helped me stay focused when I could not concentrate. She rubbed my back when I screamed aloud. "Annie, you can do this. Keep pushing and keep focused, the baby is almost here."

"What shall we name her, Jens?"

"I think you should decide her name, Annie. I will name our sons, but you name our daughters."

"Then I want to name her Mette Catherine, after your mother. We will call her Catherine so the names will not be confused."

"Then, her name will be Mette Catherine."

Mette continued to help. She was the one to show me what to do with Catherine when I thought I could not take another minute of crying and fussing. *When God takes something away, He sends someone to fill the loss.* Thank God for grandmother, Mette, who was the angel to me.

"Annie, please go out in the garden and enjoy this glorious spring day. I will watch Catherine this afternoon." Mette offered. It was not unusual to hear a tapping at my door and I would find Mette. "Annie, I have some fresh soup for your dinner. I am sure you did not get a minute to make dinner."

Mette was there for me when my tiny Mads was born three years later. Jens named our son after my father. Mette was there again when Hans was born in 1843. What a beautiful strong child he was. Mette would sit in the rocking chair and read stories to Catherine, Mads, and Hans. They loved grandmother Jasperson so much.

Mette told the children about Tivoli and Vauxhall, a new amusement center just outside the walls of Copenhagen. "Tivoli is a magic land with acres of carnival games and exciting rides like a merry-go-round. There is a small train that you can ride which takes you around the park, which is filled with theaters, bandstands, restaurants and flower gardens! At night colored lamps light up the lake, and on special nights they have fireworks. Did you ever see fireworks, children? Your mother would love all the gardens and hanging baskets full of fragrant flowers." Mette looked at me with an approving smile.

"Farmoder, please tell us another story." Hans would plead.

"Let me tell you about Shrovetide." Mette began. She carefully crafted her story telling skills to take the children's imagination to the center of town. "Just before Lent, every little youngster dresses up in a costume. They carry their own tin and go door-to- door repeating the phrase. "Boller op, boller ned, boller i min mave, hvis jeg ingen boller får, så laver jeg ballade" which means "Buns up, buns down, buns in my tummy. If I do not get any buns, I will make trouble."

Mette told the children about the traditional fun of "Cat in the Barrel." "During Shrovetide, there are lots of parties for children. They suspend a barrel filled with sweets and other goodies." Mette continued, "All the while, the children are armed with clubs, each taking their turn at knocking a hole in the barrel. The one completing the task is chosen 'King' or 'Queen of Cats'." Those days were filled with thankfulness for Mette, a great appreciation for Jens, but a constant longing for my own family. Oh, if it were possible, just for one afternoon to have all of our family together. *I can imagine it now: mother, father and Else's family pulling up in a wagon; a picnic in the garden with lots of food, laughter, children, and songs. They would be so proud.*

Four

*T*he winter of 1847 was harsh; one of the coldest in years. Winters seemed harsher when someone took ill. "Jens, it has been three days since your Moder took sick with this terrible fever. I have tried everything I can think of to help her, but the fever does not break. I think you should fetch the doctor tomorrow."

"Yes, Annie. I will go first thing in the morning. For now, Annie, we will take turns sitting with her."

As we prepared for another night's vigil, Mette looked me in the eyes and made a simple request. "Please bring the children to my room. I want to see my beautiful grandchildren."

Our little family gathered around Mette. "The children are here, Farmoder." I dare not let the children too close, but she spoke to each one, confirming her love and reminding them to be strong. We all stood together while Jens prayed for his mother. "Come with me, children. We need to leave your fader with Mette for awhile."

The night turned even darker with the passing of Mette. I thought we were prepared to lose her, but there was nothing I could do to make her passing any easier for Jens. He sat with his mother's lifeless body for the longest time. I tried to console the children, hoping that my explanation of death would be enough.

"Farmoder has gone to another place, far more beautiful than Denmark. She has gone to a place where she has no more pain, to a place called 'heaven' where she will meet Jesus." I tried to keep the explanation simple.

"Will we see farmoder again?" Catherine asked.

"Yes, I am certain that we will."

Jens talked with the children about Mette's death more than I did. "Jens, I feel so inadequate to explain death to the children. It seems as though the emotions I experienced through the loss of my own parents are right on the surface."

"I understand, Annie, but remember, we must wait on the Lord, as we do not understand His ways."

Losing Mette was far more difficult than I ever imagined. Our children lost the only grandparent they would ever know, but Mette's loss to me was tremendous. Mette was my closest friend, my parent, my confidant. She taught me how to organize my daily routine. She taught me how to bake the traditional family recipes. Jens loved Mette's pastries; and I learned to make apple strudel just as well as she did. Most of all; Mette taught me to be more patient with our children and to shower them with affection at every opportunity.

Perhaps my sensitivity to death was compounded by my pregnancy. I had approximately three months before delivery, so Jens was anxious to please. "Do not worry about getting the garden planted, Annie. The soil is still too cold." Or he would insist "Annie, please take a nap. Catherine can watch the boys for awhile."

Yern was born right on schedule, just three months after Mette passed. "He is going to be a big man some day, given the size of his lungs." Jens laughed. "Where did he get such a voracious appetite?" I struggled to keep him fed. Quite often I did not have enough milk to nurse him. I did not understand why the milk was not coming in like usual.

What would I have done without Catherine? Being the oldest, now nine, Catherine took on a nurturing role with the boys just like I remembered my sister had done with me. "Moder, I will take care of Mads and Hans while you feed Yern. You need to rest more so you will have enough milk to feed him."

Those years were very difficult, not just for our family and Jens's business, but for all Danes. Jens and I were very fortunate to have a small farm, but we were the exception. "Do not get me started about the poverty level in Denmark." Jens sipped on his morning coffee. "The monarchy owns most of the land, and those that do not own land have no chance of ever being able to rise to another class level. As the class levels become farther apart, the monarchy becomes more wealthy. The poor workers are like slaves to large landowners."

"Oh, Jens, calm down. There is not a thing you can do about the situation."

"I can not help myself, Annie. I get so frustrated with the government's oppression. Having war after war with Germany has not helped our country's financial situation. Denmark is bankrupt and the people are starving. Thank goodness, we have property and can take care of our family."

Amidst this very difficult time, however, King Frederick VII did give us all a special gift. The King signed the Constitution Act of Denmark giving civil rights to the people and limiting the monarch's power. I mention this because this Constitution gave our people freedom to worship as they desired, and a great religious movement began.

Yern had just turned two when I began noticing changes in my body. I struggled to find the energy I normally had. I was forced to rely on Catherine more than I liked. I waited and waited until I had no doubt before I broke the news to Jens. "I have not mentioned this to you before now, but I am positive I am with child. In case you have not noticed, this makes our fifth child! We are already crowded in this tiny house. Where am I going to put this new child? When are you going to build that home you promised when we married?" I was filled with emotion. Tears filled my eyes and flowed down my flushed cheeks.

Jens was calm. He never uttered a word, but he could see the worry in my eyes. "I am so sorry, Annie. You have every reason to be upset and frustrated. I should have talked with you long ago about building another house." Jens reached out, touching my arm, giving me the assurance that everything would be all right.

My face turned hot with embarrassment. "I am sorry, Jens. I should have never spoken to you with such sharpness."

Jens continued to talk about news of the war, about suffering and poverty. I did not want to give Jens any other worries, so I held my delicate condition close to my heart and thanked God every day for our family.

It was in August when our oldest son, Mads, took ill. He

was a small child, usually energetic and filled with curiosity. Mads loved to help Jens in the blacksmith shop, pumping
on the bellows to keep the fire hot. He was so small that he
could not reach the bellows, so Jens rigged up a system allowing Mads to help by pulling on a rope attached to the bellows.

At first, I did not think much of Mads' complaints. I
thought he would soon be running around the farm again.
Days passed and Mads remained ill. I plead with Jens. "You
must go fetch the doctor. Mads feels like he is on fire."
When the doctor arrived, he examined Mads and gave us
directions. "I recommend you administer cool compresses
to his body. Give Mads this medicine three times a day. He
should be well in no time at all."

The days and nights spun into one long blur. I stayed with
my first born, trying to cool his body. I prayed over and over
for him to show signs of improvement. "Oh, God. Please
have mercy on us. Heal Mads and make him strong again.
This is the son we imagine to grow into a man and inherit
our farm. Please, please, heal him."

I clung to my faith. However, during the night on August
18,1849, our little Mads turned a ghostly white and silently
took his last breath. I collapsed in a heap of sorrow over
Mads lifeless body, crying hysterically "No! No! Please,
God. Do not take my son from me." I was not prepared for
the loss of my own child.

We mourned, we prayed, and we buried Mads in the plot next
to our family in the Gauerslund Church. The next evening I

prepared dinner in silence. As we gathered around the table, we held hands and prayed. Jens said something profound. "We all have a choice. We can spend our days in sorrow and grief over the loss of Mads, or we can get up and go to work. We have other children who need our love and comfort more than ever." Jens was right; I had to keep on 'keeping on.'

I treasured the thoughts of Samuel Rutherford, a great theologian: "Ye have lost a child - nay, he is not lost to you, who is found to Christ. He is not sent away, but only sent before; like unto a star which going out of our sight, doeth not die and vanish but shineth in another hemisphere."

The loss of my oldest son affected the rest of my life. I thought there could be no greater loss than of my parents and sister, but the pain from the loss of my own child was even greater. The pain cuts deep and never seemed to go away. It seemed my smile was buried away inside Mads's casket.

Five

The three months between the death of our little Mads and the birth of our fifth child were a real test of my endurance. I struggled to keep up with the garden and field-work. When the harvest began, I was nearly ready to deliver. Catherine was forever by my side, as my protruding stomach prevented me from doing much of the heavier work. Jens fussed and watched over me with much concern. "Anne, please send Hans to fetch me if you feel any need, and do not worry about the garden. I do not see a need for you to be out there. I will take care of the garden when I finish at the blacksmith shop."

With Jens hovering over me, and Catherine helping me beyond expectations, I gave birth to another son. Without complications, exactly on schedule, the midwife helped me deliver our fifth child on November 21, 1849. Jens and I felt this baby was our gift from God to sooth the pain from the loss of Mads. This baby was very special, perfectly beautiful, with skin as soft as clouds and eyes just like mine, and my father's. "Sad eyes." Mother called them. "Deep set eyes, the distinct Hansen family characteristic."

"What shall we name him?" I asked Jens.

"I believe we should name him after our little Mads. We loved him so much." So, as people often did, we named our new baby Mads Jensen, also. How fitting, because as babies, the two boys looked identical.

Patronymics always seemed rather strange to me, but Denmark had used the custom for many years. This is a tradition of naming the child after their father's given name. Denmark passed a law years before, making surnames mandatory, and we complied when Hans and Yern were born. Most people ignored the law, and so did we when we named our baby Mads Jenson, exactly as our first Mads was named. Therefore, Mads's surname became Jensen because Mads was "Jens's son."

The struggles of Denmark did not improve, and the borders between Denmark and Germany continued to be a spot of unrest and war. "They have inducted thirty seven thousand troops to active duty, Annie. I do not think I will be called, but many young men from Sellerup will be. There is no mistake, our community will suffer the effects of the continued wars with Germany."

One of the largest battles in Denmark was the Battle of Istedt on July 14, 1850. Jens was visibly upset with the tragic news. "Military losses from this one-day battle was huge, Annie. It is reported over five thousand Danish lives to have been lost in the slaughter. Our community grieves the loss of so many of our young men. Men, whose lives have been snuffed out long before their time. Oh, I wish it were possible to right the wrongs of war. For the time being, however, we Danes must find some peace while Germany licks its wounds."

I never looked so forward to Christmas as I did that year. I wanted this Christmas to be so memorable. Perhaps we could, at least momentarily, forget the sufferings of the war, and our personal losses. Thoughts gathered in my mind, about winter's dark days. How could we make the days a little brighter?

"Catherine, I have a wonderful idea. We can give gifts of candles and cookies to the poor for Christmas. Candles are used most especially during this month to create an atmosphere of warmth and coziness. What do you think?"

"Yes, yes, Moder! We will share our candles and cookies." I was not sure we could be too generous, but it was a wonderful plan. Mads was such a good baby, and while Mads slept, Catherine and I wrapped candles with heavy brown paper, holding them together with a small red string. It was therapeutic.

Together we baked our favorite Christmas treats over the fire in a special pan. We made our favorite gingerbread and pebernodder (peppernut) cookies. We brewed my family recipe of glogg. Jens brought home a bottle of red wine from the village, and I added a squeeze of brandy and dried fruits and almonds. The house smelled wonderfully fragrant of spices once the glogg had warmed.

We cleaned everything inside the house, shaking out blankets, washing the bed coverings, dusting cobwebs and sweeping the floors. Then we cared for the animals, putting sheaves out for the birds and even our horse got a little extra grain in his crib.

Most of the celebration started on Christmas Eve, Juleaften. At about four o'clock the Gauerslund church bells began ringing, signaling the beginning of the candlelight worship. As we arrived, I could hear the sound of the church organ playing a familiar Christmas melody, it's sweet sound floating through the snowy winter air. The chapel pews were crowded with families and rows of flickering candles lined the alter with a million points of light reflecting off the windows. The Advent wreath of green boughs and candles, dancing with light, hung near the altar, representing hope, peace, joy, and love.

Our little family filed into a pew, while our friends tried to get a glimpse of our newborn son. "Look how tiny he is!" "Precious." "How beautiful." They whispered. The angelic voices of the choir filled the chapel with the music of peace and love, and the parishioners sang traditional Christmas hymns: *Joy To The World, Oh Come All Ye Faithful, The First Noel* and my favorite, accompanied like the original version on a guitar, *Silent Night*. As the voices blended in a moment of perfect harmony, my heart was filled with emotion and thanks to Jesus Christ, the reason for the season.

> *Silent night, holy night*
> *All is calm, all is right*
> *Round yon virgin, mother, and child*
> *Holy infant so tender and mild*
> *Sleep in heavenly peace,*
> *Seep in heavenly peace.*

We did not linger after worship service, except to greet Reverend Swenson and thank him for his words of hope and peace. The horse pulled our wagon, filled with our family, home for the feast that was waiting. Rice porridge was set out for the Julenisse (mischievous Christmas gnomes) so they would relent from their pranks. Jens and Hans put the horses away, while Catherine and I sat out our holiday meal. Dinner started with golden browned duck, boiled white potatoes, a thick gravy, caramelized brown sugar potatoes and pickled red cabbage.

Risalamande (rice pudding) with cherry sauce was our traditional dessert. The children savored the sugary sweetness of the rice.

We all held hands while Jens prayed and then we ate the special feast, prepared in love and filled with deliciousness. After dessert, Jens brought out the family Bible and in his commanding base voice he read the Christmas story from Luke: "And it came to pass in those days, that there went out a decree from Caesar Augustus..."

The flicker of candles danced in the children's eyes as they listened carefully to the story of the birth of Jesus, our Savior. My heart filled to overflowing, for I was truly blessed with a family of my own. Most especially I was grateful for the knowledge of the birth of that baby child in Bethlehem centuries ago.

Christmas morning came too quickly. "Moder. Are you awake?" Hans voice was soft in the dark. I turned over carefully so as not to disturb Mads who was sleeping soundly next to me.

"Yes, Hans," I answered softly. "Be patient. I'll get up and start breakfast soon."

Hans was waiting for our traditional Christmas breakfast of aebleskiver or apple slices. I could hardly cook enough of these light and fluffy spherical pancakes, and usually, the batter was gone before the children were full. The pancakes were cooked in a special pan and served with jam. "Yummm. More Moder. More." Hans begged.

Jens stood up from the table, and in his commanding

voice, he put an end to the meal. "That is enough, children. Hans, would you help me hitch up the wagon. We have family and friends to visit. Catherine and your Moder have many baskets of candles and gingerbread to deliver."

Danish Christmas Recipe
Risalamande

3 2/3 cup milk is brought to a boil
1 cup of white rice and 1/2 cup of fine sugar is added
Cook until the rice is tender, then cool.
Add:
2/3 cup of chopped sliced almonds
1/2 cup of cream sherry
1 tsp vanilla
Whip then stir in gently
1 1/3 cup of whipping cream

Six

$\mathcal{N}$ow I understand how my mother felt when she was pregnant with me. Thinking the years had passed when she could get pregnant, my mother was probably stunned when she realized another child was on the way. She must have dreaded the delivery, fearful for her life as well as the un-born child's. Mother and I had never talked about her feel-ings and fears when she was alive, but I am sure she knew the risks. The risks of childbirth were all too real for me. All I had to do was think about Else's death during the de-livery of her third child, and I got goose bumps on my arms!

I was careful not to get pregnant, even though I thought I was safe. Obviously, I had not planned carefully enough, because I was forty-three when our sixth child was born on March 16, 1852. I was sick the entire nine months, exhaust-ed and unable to keep up, and yet Mads required my con-stant attention. Catherine and Hans were in their school training during the day. I was able to keep Yern and Mads out of trouble, but unable to keep up with the responsibili-ties of the house and farm. Jens understood. He was a kind, but firm man, teaching his sons to take more responsibility on the family farm. The children knew how to care for the animals, and to plant and harvest the wheat.

I was so grateful when the day came to deliver my baby. With the help of a midwife, our last child was born. We named him after my bedstefar (grandfather), Hans Madsen Jensen. We called him "Madsen" so as not to confuse him with our other sons, Hans and Mads. Once Madsen was safely delivered, and we knew he was healthy, we were much relieved and grateful to God for his kindness and mercy. I prayed for my own health, especially that I would be able to provide enough milk to nourish another child. I prayed for our new son that he would enjoy the nourishment and grow strong.

I shall not forget that summer. We were all very busy. Hans and Yern were with Jens, working from early in the morning until almost dark. Catherine was a fourteen- year-old woman, completely capable of most cooking and cleaning chores, which allowed me to focus my energy on the babies, as well as keeping everyone clothed. With everyone doing their part, we found peace in our family, and joy in our labors.

One evening as we ate dinner together, Jens shared some news from Copenhagen. "There is a great stir about a new religion from America." Jens said. "Missionaries are in Copenhagen now and will be coming to Hammer Parish to share news of a modern day prophet." Jens called them "Mormons."

"What are Mormons?" I asked.

"I really do not know." Jens replied. "I have heard several rumors from people at the blacksmith shop. They are talking about golden plates and a book from ancient times."

"That is just not possible. Please, Jens. Do not talk again of this around the children. The idea is nonsense. Why are you confusing the children with such stories?"

Rumors were rampant and people's reactions were varied, mostly in opposition. "Blasphemy." They cried. Jens's blacksmith shop became a buzz about the Mormons, and Jens was caught up in the excitement of the "news from America."

About a month later, Jens announced. "Annie, please be open minded about the Mormons. I am very curious and I'll be going into the village tonight for a meeting at Sern Jenson's home. A Mormon missionary is meeting with some families and I want to hear what they have to say."

"Jens, while I understand your curiosity to learn more, I do not share your same interest. I am perfectly content with our Lutheran faith and devoted to teaching the same to our children. I do not want to hear these Mormons preach of prophets and America." Aware of my opposition, Jens continued to attend these meetings whenever he could, keeping the information to himself.

I thought I could avoid hearing from the Mormon missionaries, and I did not plan to have them in my home. There was no further discussion between Jens and me about Mormons until just before Christmas. One evening at dinner time, Jens turned to me. "Anne, you will need to prepare two extra plates for dinner tomorrow night. I have invited two young Mormon missionaries, Lauritz Larsen and Christian Grix to our home."

I was not pleased with Jens, and my scowl told him so. What could I do? I considered my alternatives: refusing to participate or continue to be my usual compliant self. That seemingly small decision set off a chain of events in my life that I could not have ever imagined. I reluctantly prepared extra food and served Elder Larsen and his brother, Elder Grix.

The "Elders" as they called themselves, were young brothers from the little town of Hammebund, Hammer Parish (Sogn) and sons of Lars and Anna Johansen. They were very energetic, in both their speech and appetite. They ate like they had not eaten in days, filling themselves with the meal of stew and homemade bread.

It was obvious Jens knew these men. They chided one another, laughed and enjoyed our home. Jens had listened to them preach, and he was feeling comfortable with their message. He wanted me to feel the same. "Please, Anne, just listen to them."

Their presence in our home, from the moment they walked in, was an experience like I had never known. It seemed as though the very air was electric, their voices commanding, and their message powerful. "Let us pray." I listened to their sincere prayer. "Oh, God, please send Thy spirit to be with us as we share the good news of your restored Gospel. Amen."

Elder Grix began. "Jens. Annie. The true church of Jesus Christ has been brought back to this earth through a young modern-day prophet, Joseph Smith. We bring you good news from the Utah Valley, a place we know as Zion, and the Church of Jesus Christ of Latter-day Saints."

How could this be? I had been so adamant against any Mormon discussions, but from the first night I met the Mormon missionaries and heard them preach, I believed. Their warm sincere prayers touch my heart and I felt the Holy Spirit witness the good news is indeed true. Every thought of opposition on my part disappeared.

Over the next few months, the missionaries came to our home often. They were always hungry, and I made sure they were fed before they preached to our family and other families we invited to our home.

"This is the Book of Mormon, another testament of Jesus Christ." We were presented with a new copy of the book, translated into Danish. "We just received these new translations a few weeks ago." They continued. "Joseph Smith was but a young man of fourteen when he saw a vision that was to change the world." They taught us how the gold plates were received, and how they were translated by Joseph Smith. We learned about the organization of the Church and the restoration of the Priesthood.

Elder Grix talked of the persecution of Church members and leaders. "On the dreadful day of June 27, 1844, Joseph Smith and his brother were murdered in Carthage, Illinois. Brigham Young was to become the new leader and organize the exodus from Nauvoo, Illinois to the Utah Territory.

"Saints from every nation are immigrating into the Utah Territory. They are building new cities, high in the Rocky Mountains. It is a vast territory, Jens, with free land for everyone. It is a place of freedom from religious persecution like the Saints have endured for many years."

Elder Larsen talked of a small group of "Saints" in Hammer Sogn that were meeting near his family home. "The Saints in Hammer Parish are led by my father. They call him "Father Lars." My family is friendly, honest and straightforward. They are God-fearing people, and would welcome you to their meetings."

Jens and I continued to entertain the Mormon missionaries in our home. Never could I have prepared for the reaction from our neighbors and friends when rumors began circulating around Sellerup and Gauerslund Sogn of the "Mormon" activity at our home. I was not aware of the lengthy heated discussions in the blacksmith shop until later. Old friends and neighbors threatened Jens. "You are taking your family on a fast road to Hell. If you continue to pollute our community with talk about Joseph Smith and Mormons we will force you out of business and run you out of Denmark."

The first I became aware of serious community unrest and persecution was on the day Catherine came home from school. She was sobbing. "Moder. I do not understand why you and Fader continue to have the Mormons come to our house. You do not understand what the other children are saying about us, and today a boy threw rocks at me on the way home from school."

Jens listened to Catherine, then kindly put his reassuring arm around her shoulder. "I will take care of you, Catherine. I will speak to the boy's father tomorrow. I am sure that will not happen again." Jens hesitated, then he turned towards the children. "How would you like to go to Hammebund in the wagon? Let us all go meet with a group of Saints that will be gathering on Sunday."

Seven

Our children snuggled together, with homemade quilts tucked securely around, filling the back of our wagon. Catherine held baby Madsen and I sat in front with Jens, chilled slightly from the bit of stubborn coldness hanging on from the winter. Wispy clouds filled the sky and clung to the waters around the fjord.

Jens headed towards the Johansen farm in Hammebund. This was a new route for me. I absorbed the beauty of the rolling farm fields, freshly sprouted with shoots of spring, surrounded by forests alive with blooming buds. *Denmark is truly a glorious land.*

We arrived before dusk, and with excellent directions from Elder Larsen, we found the Johansen family farm. "Hello and greetings to you from your sons, Lauritz and Christian. Jens Jasperson is my name." Jens continued to explain. "We come from Sellerup, and have been meeting with your sons, where they have been teaching us about the restoration of Christ's Church. We would like to join you and the Saints that meet on Sunday, if we are welcome?"

That was all it took, a mere mention of the young Johansen brothers and the Mormon's. We were made to feel as though we were family. "Come in. Come in. Please gather your family, Jens, and bring them into the house. We have plenty of room for you to sleep, and food enough to warm your innards." Lars smiled and motioned towards his house.

Lars introduced our family to Margrethe and their daughter, Maren. "This is Jens Jasperson and his family from Sellerup." Even though Margrethe had been caught off guard by our arrival, she was friendly and kind, quickly grabbing her large plaid apron and tying the apron strings around her dress of homespun. "Margrethe, the Jesperson's will be staying the night and they need something to eat right away."

Jens and the boys disappeared into the barn with "Father Lars" to take care of the horse, while I nursed our baby. Margrethe and Maren's hands swiftly prepared a meal of homemade bread and butter, boiled eggs and cheese, while we became acquainted. Understandably, most of our conversation focused on Margrethe's sons. "Please tell me, Annie, how are Lauritz and Christian? We miss them so."

"Your sons are quite well, Margrethe. They have been in our home many times in the last several months. We try to feed them often. I continue to be amazed at their energy, their conviction and total dedication to missionary work. Lauritz and Christian feel like part of our family, now."

"Thank you, Annie, for your kindness towards our sons. I can already tell, you and your husband are good people." Margrethe talked openly of her faith in Christ and how their family had joined the Mormon Church. "Our oldest son, John, and Lauritz first heard of the Gospel from missionaries, while they were in the military in Copenhagen. In the spring of 1851, they came home to visit and preach, converting our family as well as a small group of people from Grejs."

All the while that we stayed in the humble home of the Johansen's, I distinctly remember a powerful feeling of peace, warmth, and love. The Johansen's were that kind of people. They would have welcomed any other family, just the same. "We will need to leave early Sunday morning to gather with the Saints in Grejs." Lars reminded us. "Maren will have some Danish ready for us to eat before we need to start."

Early Sunday morning the Jasperson wagon and the Johansen wagon headed towards the village of Grejs. I was comfortable with Margrethe and Lars, but I realized how nervous I was as we approached our destination. I had never been in a meeting with Saints, other than in our own home, and I had so many concerns and questions. "There are about thirty-five Saints in our little branch." Lars told us. "These Saints come from area farms, some traveling great distances, and we meet in a large room of a woolen mill, thanks to the generous managers that we have known most of our life."

I need not have been concerned about gathering with the Saints. It was more like a family reunion! As each family arrived I realized they were just like ours, with many children. The men grouped together, talking of farms and wagons, patting themselves on the back and exchanging strong handshakes. The women, both young and old, gathered in another group, laughing and chattering amongst themselves, excited to be together again.

Margrethe was quick to introduce me to the other women. "Sisters, this is Annie Jasperson. She is from Sellerup, and comes with her husband, Jens, and her family for our meeting today. Please make her welcome." I was absolutely overcome with the feeling of acceptance and love from the other sisters. The women captured my heart as they talked about their families, sharing their excitement about a newborn child or those young adults that were already married. They shared their testimony of the Church, each one with an attitude of love and kindness. From the beginning, it was obvious that the sisters were a tremendous support for each other because not all the sisters shared the same excitement about leaving their homeland for America.

"How can I leave my parents?" Sister Thompsen cried. "Not only are they old, they adamantly oppose the Mormons. How can I leave them when I will not likely ever see them again?"

When the meeting began, I quickly realized I could not compare this worship experience to that of my upbringing. Not even close. There were no stained glass windows of an ancient building, no flickering candles, no pageantry, no formality, no liturgy and no reverend! I would miss that part. Jens did not. My voice was timid, uncertain as to the melodies of the hymns we sang from a small booklet. The booklet held about twenty songs without written music. I was told this new Mormon hymnal had recently been published in Danish.

Even though everyone spoke in Danish, Jens and I still felt awkward with some Mormon terminology. The adult members were generally referred to as 'brothers" or "sisters." Brother Johannes (John), Lars' oldest son greeted our family. "Welcome to Sacrament meeting, Brother Jasperson. So good to finally meet you Sister Jasperson. We have heard much about your cooking from Lauritz." Everyone laughed.

For hours we listened intently, with a thirst for more, and we were not disappointed. Lay speakers talked of basic beliefs, faith and baptism by immersion. Another Brother talked about the restoration of the Gospel, and the gathering of Saints in these last days. "Let all who can procure a loaf of bread and one garment on their back, be assured there is water plenty, and pure by the way, and doubt no longer, but go next year to the place of gathering, even in flocks, as doves fly to their windows before a storm."

I was keenly aware of an electrically charged atmosphere, one I had felt before. This atmosphere filled the room with power and energy as the Elders spoke of "hastening the work." They called on all Saints to "rise up for the building of Zion in the promised land." They spoke of a great valley full of promise, thousands of Saints led by a great leader, Brigham Young, and a valley filled with free fertile land for everyone. At one precise moment Jens turned directly to me, our eyes met, and although I knew I did not understand everything, I had no doubt that we were meant to be here. We were ready to be baptized.

As the wagon headed back to Sellerup, Jens and I talked about our weekend. "Jens, I felt so welcome and comfortable with these Saints. The Johansens were so hospitable."

"Yes, I agree, Annie. I loved the sermon about the 'building of Zion.' " There could be no misunderstanding what the Elders meant when they talked of Zion. They are calling on us to sell everything, the farm, the animals, and to leave our homeland for emigration to America. The building of Zion needs strong tradesman. I believe I am being "called."

Our baptism was planned for a Saturday, April 9, 1853. Several members of the Grejs Branch were in attendance, including Brother and Sister Johansen. "There is no reason to wear your Sunday dress, Annie." Sister Johansen suggested. "I would just wear your older homespun and pull your hair up into a tight bun."

I was comfortable with that decision. "Do not worry Sister Jasperson." Elder Larsen said. "I will hold you like this, with my right arm to the square. You hold onto my left hand as I immerse you in the water." In a secluded cove, our small group of Saints huddled together to pray by the beautiful still water. The Saints sang a hymn. Elder Larson spoke briefly and reminded us that it was just twenty-three years ago, almost to the day, when the Church of Jesus Christ was organized by Joseph Smith.

Jens was baptized first, then it was my turn. I was not so prepared for the frigid water. My toes were numb, and chills swept through my body. "Hold on to my arm, Annie. I will help you." Elder Larsen and I continued into waist deep waters, my body trembling from the bone-chilling water. In humility, I closed my eyes and was baptized as Christ was, by the power of "one that held the authority."

After our baptism, we usually traveled to Greis on the Sabbath to meet with our fellow Saints. The meetings were spent in song, worship, and preaching of Christ. The afternoons were spent planning our exodus. There was much to be done, and very little time to get ready, if we planned to be on the ship for America by December.

Hymn 15

Yes my native land, I love thee,
All thy scenes I love them well
Friends, connexions, happy country.
Can I bid you all farewell?
Can I leave thee,
Far in distant lands to dwell?

Home! thy joys are passing lovely
Joys no stranger heart can tell;
Happy home! 'tis sure I love thee,
Can I - can I say Farewell?
Can I leave thee,
Far in distant lands to dwell?

Holy scenes of joy and gladness
Every fond emotion swell;
Can I banish heartfelt sadness
While I bid my home farewell?
Can I leave thee,
Far in distant lands to dwell?

Yes! I hasten from you gladly,
From the scenes I love so well;
Far away, ye billows, bear me,
Lovely, native land - farewell!

(original Danish hymnal)

Eight

*M*issionaries, friends, and families from Brejning and
Sellerup crowded inside our small home. It was standing
room only. The young missionaries prayed for God's Spirit
to be with us, then they preached and taught simple funda-
mental truths from the Book of Mormon. To assume these
meetings were always harmonious and joyous would be a
mistake. Far too often disagreements broke out amongst
the men and shouts of damnation would destroy the spirit
of the meeting.

"You are teaching falsehoods, Larson! Your teachings are
contrary to the Bible." A neighbor shouted harshly.

"Joseph Smith was no prophet. Smith was a liar! God
did not speak to him, nor did angels appear with a golden
book!" shouted another.

Jens tried to keep the peace by asking all of our guests to
listen and to be open-minded. Still, too often, simple murmuring erupted into an emotional explosion. Jens's deep
voice boomed through the crowd, responding to the cri-
tiques. "Men! Men! Please keep your opinions respectful, or
I must ask you to leave our home."

For the most part, meetings in our home were orderly and
emotions kept subdued. Jens, however, was not prepared
for the relentless persecution by some neighbors, once considered as friends. Fortunately, Jens escaped critical injury

late one evening when a mob came to the blacksmith shop. They were intent on causing harm. "We warned you about your meetings, Jens. You and your Mormon missionaries." The mob pushed Jens into the corner. "You Mormons are not wanted 'round here. You understand, old man?"

Jens took a vicious beating from the masked mob. They beat Jens with wooden clubs and tore his clothing to shreds before they were satisfied. "No more meetings in our community, Jens. Do you understand? No more Mormons around here." We sought protection through legal sources, but the local magistrate informed us "there is no law in Denmark to protect Mormons."

Our weekly Sunday wagon ride to Grejs was a brief respite from the difficult tasks and persecution of the prior week. The children huddled together, sleeping in the wagon while Jens guided the horse down the road and through the fields. I relished the ride; the silence, the escape into the stillness of the land. The only sounds came from a few noisy crows and the clip-clop, clip-clop of our horse.

Occasionally we traveled to Grejs with other wagons full of families. We were eager to meet with believers and friends who fast became like family. I found strength in the circle of women "sisters." For instance, Margrethe Johansen. She was such a powerful woman. I appreciated her tender kindness, but most of all her strength. I felt so loved and encouraged by Margrethe. She was like the matriarch of all the sister Saints, speaking kindly and supportive, and ready to lift up any disheartened spirit. Any woman that felt they could not possibly join the "gathering" and forsake their homeland were strengthened by Margrethe's great testimony of faith.

Dorthea Powelson was a petite confident woman from Lihmskov, and how I enjoyed her company. Dorthea and her husband, Mads, a farmer, had a family of six children. I was about six years older than Dorthea, but our children were very close in age. Soren, Dorthea's baby, was just six months older than our baby Madsen. Catherine found a new friendship with Dorthea's daughters, Mary and Annie.

Each Sunday, as our family arrived in Grejs for worship, my eyes searched for Dorthea. "It is so good to see you again. How is your family?" We shared our joys and confidences. "Mads is not so converted to the Gospel as I would like, nor is he thrilled about selling our family farm. I am the one that is convinced of the Gospel's truth, and I am determined to join the Saints in Utah. Mads has agreed to join us, but I fear he is only going because of me."

Sister Capson was another dear friend. "What about your mother, Ingrid? How can you leave Denmark, knowing that you will not likely see your mother again?"

Ingrid was quick to respond. "Annie, I have had that very conversation with mother. Mother knows she is too old to make the trip with us, but she also understands my passion for the Gospel. Mother knows how the testimony of truth burns in my soul, and that I must follow the "call" to gather in Zion, even though we have reckoned that we will not likely see each other again. Mother wants me to go, to make a better place for my family, and she is comfortable in the care of my older brother."

There were other women in our little group of Saints equally as strong as Dorthea, Margrethe, or Ingrid. Having strong women surrounding me, along with the strength

and conviction of Jens, made my individual situation easier. I was eager to take leave and ready to start anew in the
land of promise. America! America! Not since the deaths of
Else and Mother did I feel so connected and loved by other
women.

Jens was in charge of our exodus. I trusted him. There was,
however, that little nagging desire to be in the meetings
when the men studied the maps and made all the plans. I
was given brief information regarding the route. Jens said,
"I understand your need for more details. Listen, I can
tell you that we will be leaving Copenhagen by way of the
steamship to Kiel, Germany. We travel across Germany
to Gluckstadt. We go by ship from Germany to Hull, England; and finally to the port city of Liverpool. We will sail
from Liverpool, through New Orleans, to the frontier city
of Kansas City, Missouri. It is there that we will begin the
trek across the plains into Utah Territory. There is no need
for you to concern yourself about the details because all of
our transportation has been arranged by the Church leaders
in Copenhagen. Travel from Sellerup into Copenhagen is a
group effort, and our Company is arranging for that. Once
we board the ship in Copenhagen we will be directed by
leaders at every stop that will guarantee our safe arrival into
Zion."

Jens was a businessman, and had taken care of our financ-
es since our marriage, so there was every reason to trust
him with all the financial details of our emigration. "Annie,

you need to know that our Grejs Company of Saints will be leaving on December 10 and coming this way by wagon towards Fredericia the following day. We must make sure our trunk is packed and everyone is ready early that morning."

"Yes, Jens. You need not worry. I will be ready." I paused and remembered a conversation I had overheard the prior Sunday. "Jens, I heard Sister Hansen tell some women that her family would be using a travel fund provided through the Church. Are we going to be using a travel fund to pay for our tickets?"

"The tickets are very expensive, Annie. Just one year ago the Perpetual Emigration Fund was open for Saints from Europe to assist in their passage. Some members will be using the fund for their full passage, others for a part, but they will be obligated to repay this fund through money or labor after their safe arrival into the Utah Valley. I do not expect to use the emigration fund because we should have sufficient funds for our fare, once the farm is sold.

"We need to have our tickets paid within thirty days before the steamer leaves on December 26 from Copenhagen. I am prepared to pay about fifty rigsdalers each for you, Catherine, and myself. The fare for the younger children is about thirty-eight rigsdalers each." Jens continued. "Not only will all transportation be included, but transport agents will be at each stop to make sure we arrive safely. In addition, I will prepay the expenses for our outfit of wagon, oxen, and supplies that will be available, once we reach Kansas City."

"Jens, I am so grateful for your endless labor and business skills that make it possible for our family to be included in this great journey. I pray that our sacrifice will not go unnoticed and that our children and grandchildren will someday thank us for the choices we are making today."

"Annie, some of the men do not have the money to go right now. They remain hopeful to have the necessary savings within one or two years. Meanwhile, some of the men have been asked to stay in Denmark. For instance, not all of Father Lars family will be going at this time. Lauritz, Christian Grix, and Johannes will remain behind to dispose of their family property and continue in their missionary efforts. The missionaries will also need dedicated Saints to remain behind, at least for now. Christian J., another son of Brother Lars, will be going with us because he has been called to be the president of the first emigration company of the season. Christian J. is also in charge of our small group, making the necessary arrangements for transportation into Copenhagen.

"There is a single young convert from Vejle who wishes to emigrate, but he does not have the funds to buy his own ticket. John Munsen is his name. I would like you to meet him this next week. I believe we could use his assistance when we start out from Kansas City, and unless you have serious objections, I intend to pay for Brother Munsen's ticket. I will appreciate another strong man's assistance when I start clearing our own land in Utah. John has agreed to work for us until the cost of the ticket has been repaid.

Jens continued. "There has been some interest in the purchase of our farm, but nothing has been determined. I am estimating the value of everything, the property, buildings, equipment, and animals should bring eight thousand rigsdalers. Even if we have to take a loss on the true value, we should be financially prepared by the time the payment is due for our tickets."

The December depart date wore on my mind, creating a whirl of nervous anxiety, and childlike excitement. I had never traveled farther than Grejs, and the thought of going just to Copenhagen was thrilling. I wanted to see the city of tall buildings, Fredericksborg Castle, and Tivoli Gardens while we were in Copenhagen. That was just the beginning. We would be going to Liverpool and thousands of miles beyond. I had seen sketches of New Orleans and America, and I had read about the great western migration, but this time we would be there, inhaling the clean air of freedom.

"Jens, do you have the trunk finished and ready for packing?" Not only was Jens an excellent blacksmith, but he knew wood, and had skillfully crafted a trunk for the trip. I had seen some of the construction process, built with precise dovetail joints and painted in intricate detail. Jens was extremely proud of his handiwork, and rightfully so.

Jens smiled. "I will have it done in two more days."

What clothing should I take for the children? Will we have warm enough coats and hats? I must take that quilt mother made for us when Jens and I were married. Actually, I think we need to take every single quilt we have. Shoes! I need to make sure Jens's boots are in good repair. We will want the Bible given to us by Jens's mother, Mette. I must take the garnet and pearl pin, a gift from my mother. I will wrap it in a hankie and tuck it deep in the corner of the chest. I wished I could take my good dishes, but there will not be enough room for that. Pans. I will take the Dutch oven and the iron skillet and the tin plates with knives and forks. We need a container for water. We are to bring our own chamber pot. Jens has a rifle and a shotgun that he must take. "Jennie," my precious loom must be left behind.

"Please, Jens. Before we leave could we go visit the Gauerslund Church cemetery, one last time? I want to say a final farewell to our parents and little Mads."

Nine

*T*he caravan of horses and freight wagons loaded with trunks, boxes, and large families wound through the streets of Brejning. Weighted down by layers of clothing, coats, and blankets, our company of saints took leave of our beautiful homeland. December 11, 1853, marked the beginning of our great trek into the deserts of Utah territory. We would never see our native land again.

"Do not look back, Annie." Father Lars warned. "Keep your eyes focused on your purpose."

The bans had been posted on the doors of Gauerslund Church weeks before, giving notice to our community that Jens and I were leaving. Upon the first sighting of our group moving through Brejning, many of the townspeople gathered on the streets to watch our exit. Voices of strangers and old friends alike, filled the air with jeers and such wicked language as I shall never forget. *Me thinks they made fools of themselves.* We were leaving behind very few friends, because in their eyes, our religion had made us contemptible and degraded. We had become strangers in our own community, making the leaving all the easier. Never mind the hatred. We cared not what the people thought.

The group of Saints from Grejs included Father Lars Johansen's family, Mads Powelson's family, and Carl Capson's family. They were among the caravan of wagons that stopped to pick us up in Brejning. John Munsen joined the group with our family, as agreed. The first leg of our journey was Fredericia, a port city on the sound of Lille Baelt (Little Belt) in the southern part of Jutland. Fredericia was one of the largest traffic hubs in Denmark, as well as a large military area.

"Annie, do you remember me telling you about the Schleswig-Holstein War? That day-long war was fought in Fredericia in 1849 with the Germans. We should likely pass by the newly erected memorial honoring the two thousand dead and wounded Danes from that battle."

I was astonished when our wagon train pulled into the port area of Fredericia. There was a mixture of marine traffic, dock workers, and passengers bustling about, hauling goods of every kind in all directions. Jens leaned close to me to make sure I could hear him. "We are going to ride the ferry from here to the city of Strib. That is a small ferry town on the island of Funen. There are no overnight accommodations at Strib for our group, but the brethren have arranged for freight wagons to take us to Odense. That is just another thirty miles from Strib. We will hold up there for food and a night of rest."

We were all exhausted by the time we arrived at the old lodging house on the outskirts of Odense. The house was a traditional building in Danish style with very few windows and a rickety wooden floor. The meal prepared for us was beyond my greatest expectations. "I do believe this is the best soup I have ever eaten."

Catherine blew on hers before taking another bite. "I can not decide. The soup is either extra delicious and creamy, or I am just starving."

Jens agreed. "Soup with cheese and homemade bread. This is the best. I wanted to look around Odense, just to see the retail businesses, but I believe we need to rest and make ready for an early morning departure. The wagons will take us on to Nyborg."

With the children settled down for the night, Jens and I sat close together, whispering, so as not to wake the young ones. "How are you holding up, Annie?"

"I am doing just fine. Madsen is too. He is such a good-natured baby, and as long as someone is holding him, he is happy. Jens, you never did tell me how much we received from the sale of our farm and the blacksmith business."

Jens did not respond. I studied his dark eyes, hoping to find an answer. I waited for an explanation, and then I instinctively knew; Jens had intentionally kept this business transaction a secret. "Annie, I had to sell our farm in time to pay the fees when they were due. I'm so sorry. I was forced to sell the property for four thousand five hundred rigsdalers, or one half the value I had estimated. You need not worry, though. We will have enough money to see us through."

"Jens, you allowed them to take advantage of you!" My voice grew louder. "The very people that pretended to be your friends took advantage of you. It makes me furious to think of the years we worked to make our farm productive and profitable, and then you practically gave it away."

"Hush, Annie. We must trust in God. Have faith that He will provide, and trust that His way is best. We are going with our friends and fellow saints to the land of promise. I made sure of that. I want to see Zion, just as much as you do, Annie. Have faith that all things will work together for the good."

Fresh teams of horses and new wagons waited for us to complete the next portion of the trip. "Good morgen everyone. We are ready to take you to Nyborg. It will be about twenty miles." Nyborg was a large port junction that enabled travel from one end of Denmark to the other. The harbor was overflowing with steamships, filled with exports from Funen and passenger ships filled with hundreds of people.

Upon arrival in Nyborg, we were to board a monstrous steamship headed to Korsor, a city on the large Island of Zealand. I was feeling quite intimidated by the size of the vessel loaded with products and passengers. There were no sleeping accommodations for passengers on the ship, but we followed the crowd to an area where we could stay out of the elements. "Jens, please keep an eye on the boys. I am afraid they will get lost and we will never find them! Please keep them close by. Catherine and I are going to sit here with Madsen, where it is a little warmer."

From Korsor it was about fifty miles, another long wagon ride into Roskilde, where we would go by train into Copenhagen. Our spirits were high as we traveled in the wagons, sometimes huddled together, enduring in silence, and other times spontaneously singing beloved hymns or favorite children's songs to help pass the time.

I was astonished when I saw the great locomotive at the Roskilde Station. "What an incredible giant machine." Jens stood on the platform, admiring the engine that had received so much attention in the last six years. Jens knew all about the history of The Roskilde-Copenhagen rail system. "It was built under much criticism, but by 1847 the rails were running north and south from Copenhagen to Helsinger. The newer east-west connection to Roskilde allowed quicker transport into the city for thousands of Danish citizens. No more had the rail line been completed into Roskilde than the railroad companies began public discussions to extend the lines to the port city of Korsor."

"I guess we are just a year too early, Jens. The rails are not quite finished into Korsor. The train is a marvelous piece of transportation. "

The locomotive, a black belching steam monster, pulled away from Roskilde as we found seats inside one of the cars. Still bundled up, we watched the farmlands whiz by and homes of more populated communities come into view. The locomotive stopped periodically for additional passengers, clickety-clacking along the rails, the whistle wailing through the frigid air. Our little family sat quietly; the children's eyes wide with wonder.

As promised, a small group of Saints was at the Copenhagen train station to welcome us. It was late in the day, December 14, when our luggage and families were loaded into wagons and deposited in front of barracks in the historic Kastellet, or citadel near Toldboden. Mormon leaders had arranged for the Kastellet to be a place of gathering for Saints from every corner of Denmark before our departure from Toldboden, the customhouse.

This ancient military star-shaped fortress was constructed in 1626, complete with grassy rolling ramparts and a moat. Inside the ramparts were cannons and many buildings, including military barracks, a chapel and a beloved windmill. The citadel was not an active military area, but a small military presence had always remained there.

The Kastellet was a mass of horses and wagons delivering trunks and luggage, while people scurried back and forth, filling the muddy streets between the barracks. The air was electric with energy and excitement. Friends shouted greetings and leaders barked directions. Christian J. directed our little Grejs Company to the assigned building that would be our home for two weeks. Each individual received a bed covering, and meager food rations.

"The kitchen is available to prepare your own food. Please be courteous and take turns with everyone else!" Preparing food in the kitchen could have been a disaster, but kindness and courtesy abounded, making the task quite tolerable. This was our first test for showing consideration and kindness toward each other.

"Working together, respecting each individual will be critical because you will all be traveling together for many months." President Van Cott warned. Within days, our "gathering" at the Kastellet had swollen to more than six hundred newly converted emigrants.

Each section of the people were divided into smaller manageable groups or companies. Each company had their own leadership. Christian J. was our company president. It took but one day at the Kastellet to realize how crucial it was to be organized. Every morning we gathered for prayers, singing hymns and further instructions. Again in the evening, we gathered for more prayers and entertainment.

President Van Cott spoke through an interpreter. "Listen up, Saints. It is critical that every person attend daily classes in English. I promise if you faithfully attend these classes, by the time you get to the Utah Valley, you will be able to communicate with the majority of the people."

Jens broke the sad news. "I am sorry, we will not be able to see Tivoli Gardens, because the park is not opened during the winter months." I think I was more disappointed than the children. "We can, however, visit the Rosenborg Castle. This castle is not just an ordinary castle, but it's interior is filled with beauty and opulence, remnants of a time when wealth and splendor beyond imagination were only available for a few."

Our guide gave us a brief historical introduction. "This Dutch Renaissance style palace was completed in 1624 as a summerhouse and gardens for Danish royalty. By 1700 it had become more of a museum, and in 1838 the Castle was open to the public as a museum of cultural history and great treasures."

"Hold hands, children, and do not touch anything. I want to make sure we do not miss the baptismal basin, made of pure gold, and the crown jewels on display here in the castle. You will not likely ever see anything like it again."

We walked back to the Kastellet through the gardens, white with winter's coat. I tried to imagine the fragrance of scarlet roses that would bloom next spring, and the pathways lined with carefully maintained hedges and fountains. *I wonder how it would have been to a part of royalty and have a summerhouse filled with gold? I wonder if being of royalty made them happier than we are? No, I do not think even royalty could be happier than I am today.*

Learning English came easily for the children, however, it seemed painfully slow for us older folks. Convinced of the necessity, I desperately tried to learn. I knew if I was to be an American, I needed to learn English. I practiced simple phrases over and over, but my Danish accent got in the way, making it next to impossible to properly pronounce the words. We were taught to say simple phrases, but when I tried to repeat the words, the children snickered and teased me! *Oh, Lord. I'm going to need your help on this one.*

As challenging as it was to share the kitchen with hundreds of other women, equally concerned about feeding their families, this turned out to be one of the most enjoyable parts of my day. Being in the kitchen early in the morning was the answer to the crowding issue. I woke up early. My pattern for rising early was established years before. When most were still snuggled in their bunks, I went to the kitchen. I prepared warm porridge, enough to nourish us until the late afternoon, when I would repeat the process.

During this time of food preparation, I made new friendships, some that would remain the rest of my life. Although we came from opposite corners of Denmark, under many different circumstances, we were now united in one purpose. I learned there was no lack of spirit, for there was an abundance of "all things are possible" attitude that would take us through any storm or any persecution.

One such early morning I became acquainted with Karen Nielsen, a young woman from Arnager, Bornholm, and her sister, Martha. Karen and her husband, Jens, were parents to a new baby, just three months old. They seemed an unlikely pair; Jens being older than myself and Karen in her twenties, sharing life with a newborn daughter. As we became more acquainted, however, their faith and steadfastness in the gospel became a testament to me.

"Jens was born in Bornholm." Karen continued. "He was first a farmer, and a violinist, by profession. Jens taught music for many years and was well known and respected in his community. When two Mormon missionaries approached Jens, his life forever changed. Jens wanted to know more about the Mormons, but a religious mob warned Jens that they would kill him if he ever joined the Mormon Church. One night a mob came to Jens' property, but citizens of Arnager protected him, and the mob was driven out of town.

"Jens Nielsen became the first member of the Church of Jesus Christ of Latter-day Saints on the island of Bornholm. He was baptized in July 1851. His music room became a place for Mormon missionaries to preach and teach others.

"Persecutions continued against Jens, and one night a mob came onto Jens' property and took him out to an open pasture. They whipped him, trying to get him to deny the faith, but he refused. They continued beating him until he fell to the ground, seemingly unconscious. One of them said, 'Well, he will never be able to influence anybody else,' and the mob turned back to town. However, as they were leaving, the men saw Jens raise his head. Turning around, swearing they would not leave him alive, the mob continued to beat him, and left him for dead."

"That is when I became involved." Karen continued. "I was able to give Jens the care he needed and save his life. Never again will he enjoy the good health he knew before. He is scarred with broken, numb and crooked fingers, which keep him from playing the violin. He has suffered many trials, but his faith in Christ has never failed.

"We were married in 1852 and made the decision to go to Zion. Selling the store and home was a great sacrifice, because most townspeople did not want to buy from us. With all that behind us now, we are able to be in Copenhagen, joining the second group of Mormon emigrants from Denmark."

"Karen, I am so thankful you have shared with me the story of Jens and your faith. It is friends like you, together with your faith, that gives me courage."

Our days at the Kastellet were filled with spiritual feasting. Day after day we listened to saints, like Karen and Jens, share their trials and stories of conversion. Together, our convincing testimonies bore witness of the truths being taught.

Ten

$\mathcal{T}$he whole of our camp gathered for prayer meeting the morning of December 22, 1854. This was the long-awaited day for the first group of approximately three hundred men, women and children to set sail. President Van Cott offered a prayer, petitioning God to protect these Mormon emigrants. "Our kind and generous God, we pray that a blanket of security is placed about these, your children, keeping them from all harm. We pray that all obstacles will be removed from their pathway, that they might be successful in their journey."

Our friend, our own Christian J., was called to be president and leader of the departing company on the steamship Slesvig. President Van Cott said his farewell to those that would come later, as he was going to accompany the first group as far as Liverpool.

The remaining Saints, under the direction of Elder Peter Hansen, were not scheduled to leave until the twenty-sixth. However, we could not let our friends depart without good wishes and emotional support. President Van Cott suggested that as many adults as possible, walk from the Kastellet to Toldboden to wish the first group farewell. Jens and I walked with Father Lars, his wife, Margarethe, and their family. "Father Lars, it is a such a privilege to see Christian J. called to take charge of this group of Saints. I know how proud you must be of your son."

"Yes, Christian J. is an amazing young man." Lars responded. "He is truly converted to the teachings of the restored Gospel. It seems unimaginable that we have all sold everything we own and are emigrating to America. Furthermore, I am convinced we Saints here in Denmark have been specifically "called" to come forward for the building of Zion."

Bundled in our warmest winter coverings, protected from the frigid winter of Copenhagen, we were a mighty force of people approaching the port early that morning. Toldboden was a mass of noisy ships, belching and coughing black smoke as they approached the pier. As rumored, a large group of protesters had gathered, screaming obscenities at us Mormons. Part of our group held back, and we huddled together singing songs of praise with all our might, attempting to drown out the vile language offered from the other disrespectful Copenhagen citizens.

With a long blast of its whistle, the Slesvig pulled away from the docks, laden with heavy trunks and supplies, and a multitude of excited children, anxious adults and heavy freight destined for Germany.

Jens and I were up early the next morning, fixing breakfast when we heard the news. "Did you hear, Elder Peter Hansen was severely beaten by protesters yesterday as he was returning to the Mission headquarters after the Slesvig departed."

I was stunned by the news. "Brother Hansen was not harming anyone!" I cried. "Are we not even safe to walk the streets in Copenhagen?" Suddenly a wave of panic gripped my body and I began trembling uncontrollably.

"Annie. We need to talk." Jens said. Pulling me gently aside, keeping his voice low, Jens began. " Annie, this is just the beginning. Things can get a lot worse before we get to Zion. I need to know that you are strong and firm in your decision to go to America. I need to know that your testimony of faith is unshakable and that you will not waver. If not, we need to go back. If you want to go back, I will go with you, but I want you to really ponder this situation, pray about it and let me know your decision."

No matter how hard I tried, sleep would not come. Rather than wake Jens, I climbed out of bed, wrapped myself with an extra blanket and walked out into the blackness of the star-filled winter night. I had to know with an absolute certainty that I believed. Was I willing to walk barefoot, if necessary, the face of this earth? Was I willing to stand up for the teachings I had been taught of the Mormon Church? This decision, this knowledge would affect me and my children forever. I prayed and I prayed. I looked into the vast heavens, and I pled for God's guidance. I prayed that my faith would be unwavering.

I spent much of the next day in prayer, looking for a sign. How could I be sure? *I have to know, Heavenly Father. Am I courageous enough? Is my faith strong enough to guide me through all the trials?*

My answer was not a loud voice that filled the heavens, but a voice I heard clearly in my mind. *Remember, Annie. Remember the feeling you had on the spring day you were baptized? You walked into those waters with absolute certainty that this is the restored Church of Jesus Christ.*

The day after Christmas our family was a part of the approximately four hundred, mostly Danish citizens, (with a few Saints from Sweden and Norway), anxious to depart from Copenhagen on the steamship, Elderin. As the ship pulled away from Toldboden, our family stood together on the deck, waiting for the last glimpse of Copenhagen. I tried to sing with the other Saints, but my voice was not there. Jens understood my silence. He put his arm around my shoulders, and we stood together listening to the hymns and the responding screams from the protesters. "Do not look back, Annie. Keep your eyes focused on our goal." Jens warned.

The Elderin was usually filled to capacity with goods to be unloaded at the port of Kiel, Dutchy of Holstein, towards the final destination of Hamburg, Germany. The ship had no accommodations for passengers. This time, however, the hold of the Elderin was filled with Mormons. Holed up in the stinking darkness of the ship's belly, we would travel across the Baltic Sea, about one hundred thirty-three miles and arrive sometime the next day in Kiel.

Jens searched in the darkness until he found our precious trunk, loaded with our personal supplies and treasures, and the chamber pot hanging off the side. "Over here. Come over here." Jens called. Draped upon, overflowing and braced against the trunk, our little family of seven prepared for the long night. Mads climbed on top the trunk while Hans and Yern propped themselves against the treasured box and I held Madsen tightly, comforting him from the confusion. I tried desperately to keep his little body warm. We would not know sleep, however. The constant noise of the ship's engine, working and groaning in the sea, the slapping of the salty waters against the hull, and the constant cries of children made sure that sleep was only imagined.

Kiel was a major maritime center, a sprawling natural port, and the largest port of Schleswig-Holstein District. We were relieved to rid ourselves of the Elderin, and eager to board the rail locomotive for Altona. Jens shared some local history. "Altona is a small city near the more familiar Hamburg. The Kiel-Altona railway line was just opened in 1844, just three years before the Roskilde and Copenhagen line. This rail line was the first line built in the Danish-controlled territory."

"How long are we going to ride this train, Fader?" Hans questioned.

"They tell me the travel time should be about three hours. This part of the trip to Altona will be easy, as compared to the night we just spent on the steamship Elderin!"

Even though the train was slow moving, and the clacking noise from the rails never ending, there were over thirty-seven carriages providing plenty of seats for the sleep-deprived passengers. Finally, we were able to rest.

Hamburg was a busy port, one of the largest centers for emigration, but our leaders had intentionally circumvented much of Hamburg. We were headed to Gluckstadt, just twenty-eight miles northwest. Transported in carriages and wagons from the Altona train station to Elmshorn, we would go by another rail line to Gluckskstadt, a beautiful city on the River Elbe at the confluence of the small Rhine River.

Jens and I were fascinated with the streets of Hamburg, lined with tall buildings, some reaching seven to eight stories high, pressed snugly against each other and painted in a rainbow of colors. We were not allowed to linger, as I would have liked, but from appearances, Hamburg was much larger than Copenhagen.

We arrived in Gluckstadt on December twenty-ninth, completely exhausted and hungry, only to find our accommodations dreadfully lacking. Morris & Co. furnished a well-cooked meal, with tea, bread, and butter, but our sleep arrangements were nothing but chairs and straw-covered floors of a great hall.

"This is where we are to sleep?" Catherine choked back the tears. "Lay down in the straw and sleep like a herd of sheep?"

"Hush, Catherine." Jens tried to console his daughter. "We need to make the best of the situation. It will not be long before we will be on our way."

It was true, the officials intended for our stay to be brief, but no one could have predicted the great ice storm that covered the harbor. Our plans for a brief stop turned into ten days of misery. We were all provided with one good meal a day for the first four days. No one expected the wait to be more than three or four days. Food supplies were exhausted, so we were on our own. We were held for days, sleeping in straw and filth, prisoners of a deadly winter storm.

Thanks to Jens resourcefulness, we did not go without food. Many men from our group shopped in Gluckstadt, but they drew much attention from the local merchants. One of the local newspapers published a story about the Mormons, drawing much ire from Brother Hanson. The newspaper made it seem that the housing provided was an act of humanity. "Thanks to the generosity of the Gluckstadt citizens, the poor Saints from Copenhagen have been allowed to temporarily hold up in the great community hall." That was a terrible insult against us.

Once again our leaders organized daily prayer meetings and language study groups. "We need everyone to keep busy. Sisters, make sure your bedding is picked up and folded each day. Keep the building free of trash." Every night we held prayer meetings. We shared experiences, to bolster our sagging spirits, but it was the old violin of Brother Rasmus Olsen that changed the gloomy boredom to a fest of joyous singing and dancing.

Children gathered close to Brother Olsen, fascinated by the sounds of familiar polkas. They clapped to the rhythm, and their eyes filled with delight. "This is exactly what we needed." Jens smiled. "Want to dance, Annie?"

We were finally allowed to board the steamship Tounsit on January 7th. We would travel about one hundred eighty miles on the North Sea, to Hull, England. Had we known what lay ahead of us, we would not have been so eager to board. The Tounsit, like the Elderin, was a merchant vessel with no accommodations for passengers, and we were crammed down into the shallow hold of the ship along with all our belongings. It seemed we were treated no better than ordinary freight.

"Jens, I can hardly breathe. There is coal dust everywhere, covering everything I touch."

"Annie. I do not know what we can do other than cover our noses with a scarf. We will be in England sometime tomorrow."

We had traveled but a short distance when great winter winds began to blow and enormous waves began to smash over the bow of the ship. The frigid sea water came splashing into the hold, drenching most of its passengers. "Close the hatches! Close the hatches!" screamed the captain.

All through that day and the next night, we rode the rough North Sea. We were buried in the blackness of the Tounsit's belly, tossed about like children's toys. Freight boxes, trunks, and people slid to and fro in unison. Frantic waves, and the roar of the ship straining against the sea, drowned out the high-pitched moans and cries from children as well as adults. Most of the passengers were dreadfully sick. If the sea did not make you sick, the noise of moaning and retching did. We nearly suffocated in that horrid black tomb.

When the hatches were finally opened, allowing the steam to escape, the stench came boiling out. The hold was a manure pit, full of refuse and liquid, six inches deep! Crew members drew up the filth, and we were finally able to climb onto the deck for a few moments of fresh air.

"Jens, I heard a small child perished last night. I do not know the child's name, but it could have easily been one of ours. Thank God our children are safe. I do believe that night was the hardest of my life. I thought that we would all perish together on the ship before we even reached England."

The Saints crowded the deck of the Tounsit when the Port of Hull came into view. "Look at this amazing site. I was told that Hull is on the rivers of Hull and Humber, and is a prosperous whaling center." Jens looked over the bustling port.

"It certainly does look prosperous. I have never seen such marine activity in my life. There must be thousands of ships in this port." As far as the eye could see, ships of every size and design danced in the sunshine of the sea.

We were in Hull but for three hours. We were there just long enough to exit the Tounsit, locate our luggage, and walk to the train station, about one and a half miles away. We were exhausted, black as Negroes from the coal dust in the Tounsit's hold, and starving for want of drink and warm food.

It was dusk as our group walked the English streets lined with gas lamps, exhausted from pulling luggage the whole distance. This would be the last train ride, the last leg of the trip before we set sail across the Atlantic. Never mind that I carried Madsen, crying hysterically all the way. What was I to do? I could not stop. I would not be left behind.

Eleven

$\mathcal{T}$he train ride into Liverpool, a distance of 140 miles through Selby, Leeds, Huttersfield, and Manchester, was shrouded with the veil of night. I strained through the windows to see the land of England but found it impossible. Hans, Yearn, and Mads curled up like kittens, sleeping in a seat nearby, while Jens slept soundly and I tried to comfort Madsen. The night seemed far too long, but finally, the train pulled into the Liverpool Station about three o'clock in the morning on January 10.

"Annie, I will wake the children and they can help carry our personal items. Can you carry Madsen, or do you need Catherine to help you?" Eventually, we exited the train car with our fretful family in tow.

Snow carpeted the ground, crunching under our feet, as we walked towards the train station. A sudden blast of frigid air took my breath, but what I observed was even more breathtaking. Homeless men and women, hundreds of homeless, were huddled against the exterior of the train station. There were so many people, even children, pathetically poor, nearly naked and barefoot. They unashamedly approached us as we passed. "Please, please. Can you spare a pence?"

Although we could not understand their English, we understood their pleadings. "Nej, Nej tak." Jens motioned for us to hurry past. It was extremely difficult for me to pass by without helping for I had never before seen such poverty and been unable to give.

We expected to locate our trunk, and together with our personal items, be transported to a lodging or emigrant house. However, as we walked towards the luggage area, along the deck of the train station, we came upon a highly emotional, extremely tired Mormon emigrant and a fellow train worker. "No," The brother screamed. "We will not leave this station until our belongs are found, and brought to us. Everything we own is in that trunk, and we will not leave without it."

"Please, mister, please calm down. We will bring all the luggage to the emigrant house in the morning. Please, mister, go to your lodging and find your rooms. Your personal items will be brought to you later in the day."

Jens hesitated. "I am not comfortable with this situation. Apparently, we are to leave our unsecured belongings here. It does not seem wise." Jens argued, as did others, but we were forced to comply. All of the luggage remained at the train station while we rode wagons into the emigrant houses. We were divided into two hotels, very near the waterfront. Our family was on Paradise Street, in a hotel just off The Strand.

The emigrant inn where we were assigned was a large old dilapidated building, dirty, musty and extremely cold. "We must make due without complaining." Jens reminded us. "We have privacy and a bed, which is more than we have had so far."

What the sleeping accommodations lacked, the meals made up the difference. At last, we were able to eat without restrictions on quantity. The hot strong coffee and sugar were delightful, with hot porridge and white bread with butter for breakfast. Our spirits delighted in the soup with beef and potatoes for dinner. Cakes, coffee and white bread for supper. We believed our stay in Liverpool would be brief so we would not mind calling this place home, at least until we were allowed to board the ship.

"I will be going into the city with some of the brethren, Annie. I don't expect to be gone very long. We want to look at the business district that is close by."

"Jens, I am very worried about Madsen. He seems very warm and refuses to take food. All he has taken this morning is water."

"Annie. Calm your fears. Give him a few days to adjust. I am sure he will be just fine."

In hindsight, we should not have been so trusting and naive, for when the trunks arrived every family found the luggage had been "cleaned." The trunks had been pilfered through, and many valuable items had been stolen. "Thank the Lord, my two guns are still wrapped up in the bottom of our trunk." Jens was relieved. I refolded and organized our clothing, tenderly repacking the trunk, all the while feeling the resentment boiling inside me.

"Oh no! Where is the broach from my mother?" Frantically I searched the corners of the trunk and everywhere in between. My prized possession was nowhere to be found. I realized the broach now rested in the hands of thieves as well as some of our clothing and two finely woven woolen scarves that Jens had bought for me in Grejs. *How could they? Filthy thieves!* This was our sad introduction to the dark, dirty city of Liverpool.

❧

The Benjamin Adams, the sailing ship that would take us to America, lay waiting in the port, among the other thousands of ships. Before we could board, however, we were required to pass a physical exam. The emigrant housing was turned into a makeshift clinic, and we stood in line for hours, waiting our turn. Waiting and waiting in line with fidgety children was a real challenge, especially with our baby not feeling well.

I was quite concerned about Madsen. He had not slept but cried all night. By the time it was our turn, he was finally sleeping in my arms. The physician looked at him and quickly explained, "Your baby is very ill with fever." The physician spoke through an interpreter. "Your baby will not be allowed on board, and you must wait here in Liverpool until your baby has recovered."

The physician's report did not totally surprise me, for we had been warned. "Any person found sick will not be allowed to board the ship. Those emigrants that are found ill will be grounded, and the main group of emigrants will sail without them." Now that Madsen was grounded, we had no option. Our family must all stay behind.

I was devastated. "It is one struggle after the other, Jens. Why does this have to be so difficult?"

"Do not worry." Jens reminded me. "We will find a ship. If we have to wait another month, we will find another ship. We can find our friends again once we arrive in Zion."

After all of the emigrants were examined, the physicians found the greater portion of families were grounded with sick children. Our leader, Elder Hans Olsen, called for a meeting with all the men. "We have too many children that are ill, grounding too many families, so the ship will not sail as planned. We will all wait for the ill to recover. Please consider our building under quarantine, although it has not been officially declared as such."

For the next several days Jens watched the other children while I focused all my time and energy on Madsen. In a nonstop frenzy, I tried to relieve his fever. The fever continued to rage, especially during the night, but I held him tightly, hoping that his whimpering would cease. I tried all sorts of remedies to cool his little body. I tried binding Madsen's head and feet in cold cloths. As suggested, I made a potion of lard, molasses and powdered alum for Madsen to sip. Jens was able to find a small bottle of whiskey for a cooling agent. He rubbed Madsen's body with the ointment. "I want to give him a blessing, Annie." Jens placed his hands on Madsen's head and began praying. "I bless you, Madsen, that your body will fight off the evils of this illness, and that you will be healed."

Pleading with our God, I got on my knees next to the bed and I began aloud. "Heavenly Father, have pity on us. Hear our prayers. If it is your will, please touch our son, Madsen, and heal him. Nevertheless, we trust your ways and are resigned to your will."

Late in the night of January 14 I tucked Madsen next to me in the bed, but exhaustion was the master of my mind. I had not slept for days, and I fell into a deep sleep. I am not sure how long I slept, but I awoke to a voice, whispering in my ear. "Annie. Annie. Wake up." It was moments before I could organize my thoughts, and remember where we were. Jens was trying to wake me. "Annie. Madsen is gone. Annie, our baby is gone."

"What are you saying? No! No! Please God, don't let this be so." Fear filled my body, and I reached out as if to save my baby from the grips of death. Jens had made no mistake. When I touched Madsen's little hand, I knew his life was gone. His tiny body was cool and lifeless. Jens's knees collapsed next to the bed, and we held each other tightly in our grief. "What are we going to do, Jens? How can we leave Madsen's body in Liverpool?" The thought was incomprehensible.

Jens wrapped little Madsen's body in a blanket from the bed, and I looked on, sobbing uncontrollably. My intention was not to wake the other children, but I am not so sure that my grief was quiet. "Goodbye my Madsen. Sleep in peace, my little baby."

I dreaded telling the other children. "Jens. Please. I can not tell the children. You can explain so much better than I." In his kind loving manner, Jens explained to our family that Madsen had died during the night. I held each of our children, assuring them that Madsen was with his Heavenly Father and that they would see him again. We answered all of the children's questions, their many questions, and then Jens left to find Margrethe and Father Lars.

"I must also find Brother Hans Olson. He will be at the morning prayer meeting, and he will know what we should do."

Margrethe was there in seconds. "Oh, my dear Annie. Jens told us and I came as quickly as I could." Margrethe's eyes quickly glanced around the room, finding Madsen's lifeless body laying on the bed. With tears filling her eyes, Margrethe held me tightly. "I am here to help you, Annie. I will do whatever I can to help you. Mette, my dearest. Come here." Then Margrethe held my only daughter like one of her own, gently stroking her hair and soothing her sorrow.

The angel of death stalked our camp for days, having no respect of persons, sucking away the very breath of our precious children. Within ten days, twenty-two children and infants, as well as two adults succumbed to the dreaded fever. Those days were horrific, the tension almost palpable, for us, that lost one of our own. The days were almost as disturbing for the families that did not lose a family member, for fear that their children may be next to contract the fever and succumb to the dreaded disease.

With the help of Margrethe and Dorthea Powelson, we dressed little Madsen in a soft blue dress and lovingly wrapped him in a small blanket. Margrethe sewed him inside. We Saints had no choice. We wrapped our precious children in bundles of sheets or blankets since we were unable to get burial boxes. Day after day we huddled together at the edge of a public graveyard, a pauper's field, and buried our children. We literally held each other together, physically and emotionally. We all supported each family as they buried their precious angels.

In that field of weeds, now filled with bundles of babies, I left my Madsen, to rest until the great Resurrection. I felt the arms of love, wrapped around me in many shapes, kinds, and colors. I would forever find the memories of Madsen's giggle pressed firmly in my mind, and the hours I had spent rocking him, patiently watching his tender face as his eyelids grew heavy with sleep.

Life is like a garden, I thought. My garden was first filled with patches of impatience, but with a great amount of effort and struggle, my garden now flourished with blossoms of patience. Once my garden had been choked with insecurity, but with help and support from friends and family, planted firmly around me, I now felt increased strength and confidence. I more fully understand that nature and life are miracles, but sometimes you have to let go. What is my reward? Love is the reward, and I have tasted the sweet nectar of love.

Twelve

$\mathcal{M}$orning prayer meetings were routine, and while we were in Liverpool, the routine did not change. These meetings not only provided a place for further instruction and inspiration, they were a place where feelings were aired and a vote of mutual consent regarding our affairs was taken.

It was still early when Jens returned with Hans and Yern from the prayer meeting. Hans rushed through the door, "Mother, mother! The ship is ready to go!"

"Yes, it is true," Jens confirmed. "They will start boarding passengers in the morning. We are told the process of loading the ship with freight, luggage, and emigrants will take several days."

After successfully passing a second medical examination, our family anxiously boarded the Benjamin Adams on January 22, 1854. Originating from the port of New York City, the Benjamin Adams had been moored in Liverpool for over two weeks, waiting for our group of Saints. She was a beautiful ship with three masts, three decks, a square stem and an intricately detailed billet-head.

"Families! Listen carefully! Go forward to the center of the steerage area and locate your family bunk. After you have located your sleeping area, locate your belongings and trunks from the upper deck. Take your luggage to the steerage area next to your bunks, otherwise you will find them in the hold. Single men! Single women! Listen up! Men must bunk in the forward area, and single women must bunk in the rear, separated by the family groups."

Although the majority of our company was Danish, a small number of Saints from Ireland, Scotland, Germany, and England had joined us, swelling our passenger list to 384. The larger part of our group was complete families, but there were a great number of young adults traveling alone. Families, unable to buy but a single fare, chose a young family member to emigrate, to find work, and send money home for the next family member to follow. For this reason, the area designated for "singles" was extremely crowded.

We were directed through the chaos of people and freight to the section known as "steerage" or what we called the "tween deck." As we climbed down the stairs to the area just above the hold, we saw nothing but an enormous open room filled with rows of bunks in dormitory style. The bunks lay in the direction of the ship, fore to aft, and there was a small corridor separating each row. The individual bunks were about 70 inches in width and length, roughly built with no mattresses or coverings. The ceiling height was about six feet, and the deck of the steerage was very primitive. In some cases, the boards were so far apart small items could fall down into the hold where the baggage was stowed away on top of the cargo.

"Annie, I am taking Hans and Yern with me to locate our trunk. We can use the trunk for a table, and it will be convenient for food storage instead of having our items in the hold. Besides, our food will be safer next to us." Jens continued. "Now boys, come with me so we can get our first weeks rations."

The Benjamin Adams was registered in the United States, and new laws had recently been implemented that required each passenger to receive specific amounts of food supplies. "We have all of our food!" Hans announced as he returned, carrying a bag of biscuits. We have two pounds of white bread, two pounds biscuits, oatmeal, wheat meal, sugar, salt, molasses, tea and three gallons of water."

"This does not look like a lot, but we are charged to make these rations last for one full week." Jens reminded us, again, about murmuring. "Even though the rations seem meager, or if we do not like what we are given, we are not to murmur or complain. Do you understand, children?"

Families continued to come aboard, filling the steerage deck to bulging. Once we were settled in, we could return to shore, if we chose. Jens bought several items from town, food items, particularly bread. He bought clothing to replace the items stolen from our trunk and soap for laundry. Jens assisted other brethren in buying a large quantity of inexpensive canvas. "We will be using the canvas for tents and wagon covers, once we arrive in America." Jens explained.

The steerage deck became our home as well as our sanctuary. Early every morning we were awakened by the sound of a trumpet, announcing a new day. Before we ate, everyone was expected to meet on the upper deck, dressed for morning prayers. We sang songs of praise, with a joy and excitement that we had never known. It was on Thursday, January 26, at the morning prayer meeting, we were told the ship was ready to depart. "Tugs will be here early in the morning to tow us out of the harbor. You might be aware, however, that not all of our Saints are with us." Elder Olson continued. "There are fifteen brothers and sisters that remain too ill to travel. Let us remember to keep them in our prayers."

The morning fog hung low on the water, and hundreds of screeching seagulls floated about the harbor, as tugboats began pulling the Benjamin Adams away from the pier. A handful of first-class passengers and 384 Saints were standing on the great deck as the ship went into motion. There were artisans of every kind: carpenters, school teachers, carriage-makers, tailors, weavers, shoemakers, stonecutters, a former Baptist lay-preacher and a good many farmers. In their native tongue they raised their mighty voices singing praises to our God. I was filled with a flood of emotion, thankful that I was witnessing this moment, but choking back the grief that was so fresh. I was leaving part of my heart behind with Madsen, buried in the icy soil of Liverpool. My voice was not there. I could not speak, nor could I sing. I could barely breathe.

In the midst of my sorrow I felt an arm slip around my waist, and through my tears I beheld the kind, beautiful, Karen Nielsen holding her own baby, Martha. Karen's soft voice spoke volumes as she held me tightly, and whispered, "I am so sorry, Annie." Suddenly I felt so blessed, for in the moments that I needed to be strengthened, when I felt my legs were not able to hold me through the sorrow, God brought me strength through friends. At the perfect moment, Karen gave me the love and support that I needed.

From the deck of the Benjamin Adams, the port of Liverpool took on a totally different appearance. Our family stood on the main deck watching tugs pulling our ship down the River Mersey, past hundreds of piers and thousands of ships. It was a magnificent site to witness. After towing us about two miles into open waters, we were left to the mercy of the winds.

The morning trumpet summoned us at 5 o'clock, and before breakfast we were all on deck, excited to view the day and receive further instructions. "Are we ever going to start sailing?" Catherine's sigh of frustration was understandable.

Normally we would have been pleased with a beautiful clear day, like this, but this day the President began, "Please, Lord, provide us with steady winds." Elder Olson then began the arduous task of organizing the Saints. He continued. "Prayer meetings will be held mornings and nights, weather permitting. Harmony and cooperation throughout the voyage are critical. I promise you great blessings from the Lord if you are obedient to the ship's officers, and the rules of conduct within our own people. You were each given a copy of the ship's rules to read. Now I am asking each of you to raise your right hand to the square, indicating that you will live by and support these guidelines."

"Yes." Loud and proud, we raised our hands, unanimously agreeing.

"If anyone is so inclined to complain," Elder Olson continued, "please raise your hand right now! I will gladly appoint you as the official complainer for the duration of the voyage." I chuckled, as did most of the group, but we knew the seriousness of the message. We were to work together at all cost.

The emigrant Saints were divided into five groups, which were referred to as "wards" and each ward had an appointed president and two assistants, as well as selected individuals for specific tasks. Each ward "called" or appointed individuals to supervise the cleaning of the quarters. Every morning before the emigrants awoke, the cleaning crew would pass through steerage, pick up any trash, and clean areas of filth. Each ward also called "captains" to help distribute provisions and ration water.

"We will be assigning numbers as to the order in which you may receive additional provisions, have your food prepared, or do laundry. Laundry buckets can be found on the upper deck, but you must provide your own soap. Brothers and sisters, cleanliness is paramount. It is important to wash your whole body at least once a week and change your bed linen as often so that peace is preserved and sickness kept at bay. We have arranged with the ship's captain to have washing day twice a week, and you may hang your clothes on the upper deck to dry."

Additional instructions were given regarding the kitchen and food preparation. "We have two different galleys; one for first class passengers only, the other for steerage passengers. Keeping in the sequence assigned, you will take your items to be cooked in your pots in the steerage kitchen. Wait for your food to be cooked, and then gather your food promptly, and return to the steerage area for eating.

"Do not stay isolated in steerage, but move about the upper deck as the sea allows." We were told to wash and comb our hair on the upper deck to prevent uncleanliness down in the ship. We were admonished to look after this very carefully and to help those that were sick, who could not help themselves. Guards were called from each ward to protect the Saints, particularly the single women from the sailors, who seemed to take delight in annoying and insulting us in every way possible.

The captain, a short, fat, fussy, old fellow, in spectacles, seemed pleased to be carrying Latter-day Saint emigrants. The captain spoke briefly at a meeting. "It is a well-known fact that for many years, no ship has been lost between European parts and America while carrying Mormons. I would say that carrying Mormons is the best assurance of a safe trip."

For seven additional days, the ship was anchored in the still waters while leaders continued to organize affairs. Although anxiety began stirring amongst the Saints, I felt a calmness and peace. The air was warm, like a Denmark spring, as Catherine and I walked about the upper deck without a jacket or shoes. "Catherine, I can scarcely believe in a few more days you will be sixteen. I want you to know, if something should happen to me or your father, you have been such a blessing to us. You are a woman now, with dreams of your own, and I pray that you will find much happiness with the Saints in Utah Valley."

"Moder." Catherine turned and looked me in the eyes. "I want you to know that I love and admire you beyond measure for your tenacity and courage. You are the strongest woman that I know, and I pray that I can be exactly like you."

"Oh, my dear Catherine. You are so precious." I smiled and squeezed her hand, but I did not agree. *She must be thinking of someone else. I know strong women. Margrethe and Karen are courageous, strong women. I pale in comparison. Least of all women, I am not deserving of such recognition.*

Thirteen

We prayed. We fasted. We waited for winds, but the winds did not come. The answer to our prayers, however, did come when a large steamer came to our rescue on February 2nd. The steamer was able to tow the Benjamin seventy-six miles further into the Irish Sea! The day after the steamer left us, winds started blowing, gentle at first, but make no mistake; they were winds! "Hoist the sails! Hoist the sails!" The deck, once calm, became a flurry of activity as the crew scrambled about, making ready the sails. One by one, 19 gigantic white sails were lifted to catch the steady winds, flying like great pillows amongst the thickening clouds.

By evening the winds began to blow with an intense fury, as if they needed to make up for time lost, rocking and bouncing the ship about like a child's toy. For the second time on our journey, we were held captive by a monster storm. We were fearful, once again, that we might perish at sea. Mountainous waves held us prisoner in steerage for two long days while we held to each other in our bunks with seasickness as our unwelcome companion.

Gas lamps were not allowed to be lit during the storm's rampage. The hatchways were covered, and the only light we knew filtered through skylights in the deck, during the day. The winds were relentless and the chamber pots and cooking utensils, held in place by a rope, clanged and danced in wild confusion. Our tinware and water bottles dropped from nails overhead and our luggage broke lose, chasing each other from side to side over the decking. Provision boxes danced about and the overwhelming stench of spilled chamber pots and lack of fresh air was staggering.

Constant jousting of the ship prevented most passengers from even standing. Brother Larsen fell and knocked his arm out of joint while trying to use the latrine. This was the first of many accidents as land legs gave way on the slippery decking. During the most violent heaving of the vessel, a number of beds or bunks, loaded with people, fell down, spewing people, boxes, and valises about in the ship.

Jens and the children seemed to adjust to the constant motion, but I was unable to shake the seasickness. We had nothing to ease the suffering.

Sunday morning the winds calmed, allowing us to escape from the steerage area. The trumpet sounded, the hatches were opened and the long task of cleaning the filth from the steerage deck began. Everyone cleaned their own bedding, we organized our area, and minding the ship's rules, we set about cleaning our bodies on the upper deck, with cold seawater, in preparation for morning prayer meeting.

"Catherine, please hold your moder's arm and help me get her to the upper deck." Jens found a sheltered corner for me to rest, away from the winds. "I am going to find you some warm bullion soup, Annie. Meanwhile, Catherine, I will need you to start washing our bedding and clothing."

The dark cloudy skies gave way to glorious sunlight and I inhaled; slow, deep breaths of salty air. Our leaders prayed and we sang songs of praise. It was no ordinary, casual prayer meeting. It was a mighty, spirit-filled meeting of sincere, thankful emigrants, raising their voices in thanks to their God for deliverance from the mighty storm.

Elder Olson continued. "I am sure that you are aware of how crowded and uncomfortable the sleeping section has been for the "single" passengers. This was made most evident during this past storm. Several brethren have since inquired of me, showing their desire to unite in marriage, thereby moving into the family section for sleeping!" Elder Olson smiled and winked. "I have approved their requests, and this afternoon we will have a wedding party for seven couples!" Smiles and cheers of approval filled the air.

The afternoon was filled with laughter, music, dancing and celebration on the upper deck. I was appreciative of the social activities, but I could only notice Catherine. She watched with innocent eyes while young couples held each other, dancing and cheering together. "This is so exciting, Moder. I have never seen such a celebration."

Where have the years gone? I have been so busy, I hardly noticed that our Catherine is no longer a child.

Sudden long blasts from the ship's horn interrupted the violin's polka. "Ship on starboard. Ship on starboard." Floating without men or sails, a lonely ship hauntingly tossed in the sea. The ship appeared to have no life or activity on board. Was this a ship broken by the storm's rage? Were the passengers swallowed up in the sea? Would the Benjamin Adams find the same dreadful demise? My fears were resurrected.

When night came, so did immense waves and mighty winds. The hatches were closed and again we were held prisoners of the steerage deck while the storm battered us about. The darkness was black as a tomb, however, the incessant noises of the storm and the cries from the sick and screaming children were not as frightening as the previous storm. Jens and I lay in our bed, encircled with our family, clinging together and praying for the night to end.

In the middle of the chaos and blackness, I heard a very familiar piercing sound; a scream not of a child. I knew the voice. It had to be Sister Anderson, a young woman whose first child had chosen this storm-filled, blustery night to be born. There were no physicians to summon, no midwife to call, and for that reason, plans had already been made to help this dear sister through a personal private experience in a place that was anything but ideal.

A single gas lamp flickered in the darkness and brethren shoved four trunks together, none of which were the same height. The makeshift table, although uneven, became large enough for Sister Anderson to use as a birthing table. Pitching back and forth with the storm, several sisters held up blankets as best they could, providing only a slight amount of privacy. An older, more experienced sister, became a birthing coach, guiding Sister Anderson through a long painful labor.

The night was never ending for those continuing to fight nausea. The steerage compartment was filled with relentless noises, but the screaming and moaning from Sister Anderson took center stage. Finally, at dawn, with the wisps of light glowing in steerage, there was one last bloody scream, followed by the distinctive sound of a newborn baby's cry. The stifling air of steerage was filled with cheers of relief and congratulations. It was as if we had all given birth to Sister Anderson's baby! "It's a boy, Kirstine. You have a new son." The baby cried and Kirstine held her son. The winds knew no reason to diminish.

Intense winds from the Northeast continued for several days, making for good sailing. We were relieved to see several of the sick ones on deck again. Most emigrants became accustomed to the constant swaying, while others remained ill, moaning in their beds and finding no relief with man's remedies. We first became aware of an older sister, Dorthea Jensen, who was suffering from a severe case of seasickness. Dorthea, unable to get out of bed, unable to keep broth or any liquids on her stomach, was critical. On Friday, February 10, Sister Jensen quietly slipped from her restless slumber to her eternal home.

Unlike the noisy heralding of our newest emigrant child, death silently stalked our ship, making no distinction of man, woman or child. As we gathered for morning prayers we were all informed. "Sister Dorthea Jensen passed away during the night, and we have gathered to bid her a final farewell." Brother Olson continued with prayers while Sister Jensen's family held each other, mourning such a personal loss of their family matriarch.

Elder Olson preached from 1 Corinthians, Chapter 15. "Oh death, where is thou sting? Oh, grave where is thou victory." He preached of life eternal and the Resurrection, assuring us that Sister Jensen's spirit now lived in a more beautiful place. "We must keep each other spiritually strong." Elder Olson concluded. The body of Sister Jensen was wrapped in a blanket, covered in canvas and tied with a rope. Several men lifted the large rough plank, walked to the edge of the deck and with one swift motion, the body slipped off into the depths of the black sea.

It is difficult for me to understand how the days melted together and we became accustomed to our circumstances; circumstances that were anything but normal. Most passengers grew accepting of the winds, sometimes blowing steady and other times with mighty force. Death, birth, and celebration visited the ship, becoming familiar, almost routine. The following week we knew the best winds we had ever known, and we also stood on the great deck and prayed for the soul of another emigrant as their body was entombed in the sea. We knew another sleepless night in steerage as a young mother gave birth to her child, and again we celebrated on deck with another young couple as they said their marriage vows to "cherish and love until death you do part."

Fourteen

Think not when you gather to Zion,
Your troubles and trials are through;
That nothing but comfort and pleasure
are waiting in Zion for you.
No, no, 'tis designed as a furness
all textures to try to consume
all the wood, hay and stubble,
the gold from the dross purify.
Eliza R Snow

"*K*eep busy, everyone. Weather permitting, all men, women and children should be working on the great deck." Our leaders made sure the decks were cleaned and swept daily. Each morning the chamber pots were lifted overboard and dumped into the sea.

"Make sure, Hans, that the winds do not catch the contents and spray back on to you or the ship."

"I understand, Moder. I will not make that mistake more than once."

Laundry days were a real challenge. Large barrels on the upper deck collected rainwater, to be used for washing clothing and bedding. Catherine and I scrubbed our clothes in our own bucket. "I think those clothes should be clean enough. Let us rinse them out, and we can drape them over the deck lines to dry."

"Do we need to stay here and watch the laundry until it is dry, Moder?"

"Yes. That is a good idea. If you will stay here, I will go check on Jens and the boys."

Usually, it did not take long for our laundry to dry, however on occasion our clothes did not dry for several days. For that reason, I never did wash some of our heavier clothing, like my dresses.

Many days were spent cutting and sewing the linen canvas brought from Liverpool. The canvas was sewn into tents and wagon covers, then waterproofed to be used when we crossed the plains. "This is really tough." Jens pushed a large needle with thick thread through multiple layers of canvas. "My fingers are raw from pushing this needle back and forth. I am going to inquire of Brother Larson if we have tools that might make it easier." Catherine worked just as hard as any other adult. The three boys played with other children, under our watchful eye.

One of the most challenging tasks of the voyage was getting a warm meal prepared in the galley. After prayer meetings, I returned to the steerage area, portioned out the grain and liquid into our pot, and found my place in line next to Dorthea Powelson, my dear friend from Grejs. We were towards the last of the line, which had its own disadvantages, but these hours proved to be the precious time for sharing our frustrations and strengthening each other.

"How are your children holding up, Annie?"

"The children have adjusted to the ship just fine, but I worry about Mads. He has eaten very little the past two days."

"You need to watch him. Find something that he will eat."

"How are your children?"

"I am telling you, it is really difficult to keep Soren out of trouble. He is climbing on everything and constantly getting into trouble. I can not take my eyes off him for a minute. I am afraid he is going to get injured."

"I understand. Mads is the same way."

Our concerns were like every other mother's concerns; keeping our family safe and healthy. Occasionally we reminisced about Denmark.

"Remember how difficult we thought our lives were in Denmark?" Dorthea snickered. "It was easy then, compared to what we are going through now. It is so hard just to get a bowl of warm porridge! We wait and wait in line for our pot, only to find the food is usually burned and inedible when we get it back!"

Finally, after more than an hour, it was our turn in the galley. The kitchen was about six by twelve feet, which housed a temperamental sweaty Irish cook. Dorthea and I tuned our voices to whispers, so as not to disturb the cook. If we stayed quiet we were hopeful our pot would get the necessary attention. Depending on the day, and how strong the winds were, many of us would only go through this process once each day. If the weather was foul, we might wait several days before we returned to the kitchen for warm food.

My friendship with Dorthea was such a treasure, but the thought of going to the galley filled me with apprehension. The process was long and tedious, and often I decided facing the abusive old Irish cook was more than I could endure. The longer we were at sea, the worse the cook became. Little did we realize a war was brewing between our galley's cook and the cook for the first-class passengers and crew members. This dispute erupted before our very eyes one day on the main deck.

I was working with several sisters, finishing the last of the wagon covers when a great commotion began. We could hear two men shouting and cursing at each other. "I wonder what is happening?" Dorthea whispered to me. Without a means of escape, we were stunned to see the ship's two cooks strip down to their waist, and with heavy blows, they began plummeting each other about the head and body. The blows continued with the cooks wrestling and rolling on the deck, paying no mind to the audience.

The women were horrified, trying not to look at the bloody mess smeared across the bodies of the cooks; trying not to listen, but without choice. I closed my eyes and looked away, disgusted with the savagery, but the racket and brutality were inescapable. Trapped in the corner of the deck, we were a forced audience to a grudge match that went on for about one hour. Then in total exhaustion, the cooks lay motionless on the deck, unable to continue, and the battle was over. I never knew if the supremacy of the galley was determined that day, but I did notice that after the brawl, our cook lost a great deal of his bitter attitude.

When we did not have warm food we relied on a small portion of dried meats, which were part of our weekly rations, and biscuits. I am sure when I speak of biscuits you might think of a light, soft bread, warmed with butter oozing down the sides! Nej! Our biscuits were called "sea-biscuits" or "hardtack" and were made of flour, water and a pinch of salt. When baked, the biscuits were so rock hard they could be used like a hammer! Sea-biscuits could not be eaten 'raw' without damaging your teeth, so we soaked them in water, coffee or tea before eating. The sea-biscuit was the main staple, with the ability to last for months, even years, providing they were sealed properly.

"Eww. That is disgusting. I am not eating that biscuit." Catherine dropped her breakfast, spilling her tea across the makeshift table. "There are critters crawling inside."

"Do not be a baby." Hans grabbed the biscuit. "The bugs might give it a little flavor."

Our spirits were lifted with the announcement of the wedding of Margrethe's son, Soren. "Brothers and Sisters. I am pleased to announce the marriage of Soren Larson to the love of his life, Maria Fredericksen. They will be wed on March 1st." Maria and Soren first met when we gathered in Copenhagen, so their marriage was no surprise to most of us women. From the time Soren and Maria first met, they were usually together, except when the lights went out at night. We prayed for weather that would allow everyone to celebrate the occasion on the great deck.

On Wednesday the winds blew at a comfortable pace, the sails were full, and we stood on the deck waiting for the wedding ceremony. "Look, Moder!" Hans pointed to the dark blue waters below. "It looks like flying fish!"

"That is amazing. If I did not look carefully, I would have thought they were birds near the surface of the water."

The fish was white, about twelve inches long with a pointed head, flying about fifty yards before entering the water again. Sea life was abundant, and no matter how often we saw the flying fish or schools of dolphins, the children took great delight in their presence.

Friends and family pushed together, making sure they could hear President Olson. "Brothers and Sisters, we are gathered to witness the marriage of Soren and Maria, who come of their own free will to unite in marriage. If any man objects to this marriage, let him speak now, or forever hold your peace."

Soren and Maria held hands, eyes fixed on each other and joy radiating across their faces. My thoughts were transported back to a day long ago in the Gauerslund Church when Jens and I promised to love each other for the rest of our lives. Since my wedding day, I had seen many changes, and we had endured many trials. I wished for Soren and Maria an easier life, a life of promise and peace in the land that we would soon call our own.

Brother Rasmus Olsen braced his feet against a heavy chest of rigging and began playing his violin. The air filled with the piercing sounds of the strings and our spirits soared higher than the sails. We danced like there was no tomorrow; bouncing, singing and clapping to the spirited rhythm. It was a grand afternoon.

No one expected refreshments. Our rations were so meager, that using them for a celebration such as this, was out of the question. "Oh, my stars and garters! Moder, they are passing out sea-biscuits and bacon! Can you smell the bacon?" The aroma of fried smoked bacon was intoxicating. I gently soaked my sea biscuit in tea, broke off a piece, and chewed the biscuit with the crunchiness of the bacon. The taste was divine. Bacon was one of my favorite foods, but having such a treat in the middle of our voyage made the celebration even more exceptional. Margarethe had performed a miracle, or perhaps she had bribed the captain, for I knew not how she found such a treat.

The festivities continued as Maria was tied to a handcrafted chair and hoisted on the mast. Maria smiled and waved her white handkerchief as she blew in the breeze. The Captain smiled. "She's a mighty brave woman, that Maria." With Maria waving in the wind, four bachelors lifted Soren high above their heads on a chair and paraded him about the ship.

During the evening prayer meeting, we were given instructions for the following day. "When you wake in the morning, everyone is to take your trunks, your bedding, everything you own to the great deck. Once that has been completed, I have asked several men to help sweep, scrape and wash the filth off the steerage deck. After this has been accomplished the ship's crew will smoke the steerage area before we return with our belongings. We have lost five children on this voyage, and we will not lose another. Everyone is to remain on the upper deck for the duration of the day while we smoke and fumigate the area. We will be back in steerage by evening."

Deep cleaning the decks usually occurred three times each week, but the fumigation was not so routine. After the decks were cleaned and washed, the crew burned pots of tar down in the steerage area, creating a thick fog that hung around for days. Smoking the room did rid the air of foul smells, but breathing the smoke was toxic.

The day when all our belongings were on the great upper deck, I particularly noticed how lethargic Mads was behaving. Even his little face was flushed and warm. Mads had not been eating like I thought he should, but this day I became more concerned.

"Jens. Does Mads feel warm to you? Do you think he has a fever?"

Jens placed his hand on Mads' head, then his face, feeling, feeling, for a fever. "Yes, he does seem rather warm. I will see if I can find Margarethe for you."

My worst fears were confirmed when Margarethe examined Mads. "Yes, I agree he has a fever, Annie. We must do everything we can to get his fever down." I was no stranger to taking care of sick children, but this time was different. The memory of losing Madsen was too raw; the memory too painful to think this could happen again.

With Margarethe's assistance, we tried all treatments known to us for fever and dehydration. We applied cold packs, but it was dehydration that seemed to make Margarethe most concerned. "You must get Mads to take more liquids. Give him as much liquid as possible."

"Jens, could you ask Brother Lars to come and give Mads a blessing."

"Yes, Annie. I will fetch him."

Brother Lars prayed with a power from on high, while Jens held our youngest son in his arms. I watched as the two men prayed together, administering to my youngest son. I was filled with faith that Mads would be healed. However, I knew Mads' life was in the hands of God. I could do everything in my power to help Mads, but life would be taken or spared by God, according to His plan.

"Drink, Mads. Please. You must drink this broth."

By evening we were ordered back to the steerage area, still thick with toxic smoke. Jens and Catherine placed our items back into the same location, made our family's bed, and Hans and Yern climbed in the back. I placed Mads next to me in the front of the bunk, and the lamps were extinguished for the night.

I did not sleep. I prayed. I held Mads next to me and I pled with God. "Lord, if it is Thy will, please Lord I pray; remove this fever from Mads's body." Then, in a soft whisper, I began singing to my child. "Think not when you gather to Zion, your troubles and trials are through."

Fifteen

Think not, when you gather to Zion
That all will be holy and pure,
deception and falsehood are banished,
and confidence wholly secure.
No, no; for the Lord our Redeemer has said
that the tares with the wheat must grow
'til the great day of burning
Shall render the harvest complete.
Eliza R Snow

*I*n the pitch black of night, I searched for sleep but failed. I hummed lullabies to Mads and held him close. I prayed for him. I prayed for his healing. When doubt crept in, and fear caused me to quiver, as it sometimes did, I tried to fill every corner of my mind with faith and hope. I pled with my God. "Heavenly Father, please hear my prayers. Heal our son. We love him and need him in our family. We have already lost two of our children, please do not take another."

Near morning, in spite of my pleadings, I felt Mads's life slip from his body. Free from his suffering, his spirit passed through the main deck and took flight into the clouds. I lay numb and motionless, unable to let go. I tried to imagine a reunion that might be taking place with Mads and our heavenly family. This time I knew there would be no final preparations, no washing or dressing of Mads's body like we did with Madsen. I waited until slivers of a new day began to slip through the hatch opening; only then did I stir Jens. "Jens," I whispered. "Wake up."

"Is it Mads?"

"Yes. Please help me."

Jens carefully lifted Mads' body from our bed, wrapped him in his arms and climbed from steerage to deliver our child's body to President Olsen.

"Brothers and Sisters," President Olsen continued. "It is with great sadness that I must tell you, Jens and Annie Jesperson's four-year-old son, Mads Jenson, died during the night." President prayed with the saints, read from the scriptures, and offered words of comfort and encouragement. The congregation sang a hymn, but I did not hear a word. My body was filled with agonizing pain.

Jens and I clung to our children, hoping to somehow shelter them from what was to come. I stared motionless at the bundle holding the body of Mads, tied in canvas, laying on a box usually reserved for rigging. From long ago I could hear Else's voice whispering in my mind. "Annie, remember, the Lord giveth and the Lord taketh. Blessed be the name of the Lord."

The process of a sea burial was familiar. We had watched grieving families mourn the loss of their children too many times. This time, however, it was my son. This time it was Mads's body that was lifted on a rough plank, weighted down with metal, and slipped off into the depths of the sea.

Once again Jens found himself trying to explain death to our little family. The finality of death is difficult to understand, but most especially for children. Our children were no different. We huddled together, and I listened to their questions, our innocent children's questions, about death and their little brother. I listened to the gentle explanations of Jens. Stepping to the side of the ship, I watched the canvas bundle sinking into the depths of the blackness. Strange how I found no more tears. Was Mads really gone?

Catherine reached for my arm, tears of loss smearing her face. "Moder, are we all going to die?" I understood her concerns, and I understood her fears, but I could not answer. I suddenly felt quite ill.

"Annie, I am here to help you." Margarethe's voice was intentionally loud. "You fainted, Annie, and you have a gash on your head. I am trying to get the bleeding to stop." Margarethe was confident in her actions, pressing a wet cloth on my forehead. "You will be all right, Annie. The laceration is not as large as we feared." Margarethe continued, "Jens, would you take Hans and Yern for a little walk. I will take care of Annie."

"Margarethe, how can I help?" Dorthea bent over, peering at my head.

"I believe Annie is fine, Dorthea. Would you help Catherine?"

"Of course." Dorthea did not hesitate. She wrapped her loving arms around my young daughter. "Do not cry, Catherine. Hold on to me. I am here to help you. You will find that many of the women will be here to support you and your family. It is okay to cry, but do not ever believe you are alone, for God will give you strength to survive your trials."

With Jen's approval, I stayed in our bed for several days. My body was racked with pain and my heart so filled with sorrow. I believed climbing the stairs to the upper deck was impossible. Catherine was there for me. "Do not worry, Moder. I will go to the galley and get our food prepared." Jens watched the two boys and kept me informed of any news. Margarethe and Dorthea were there, visiting at my bedside at least once a day.

Perhaps I could have ignored my grief and joined the prayer meetings, but I did not. The aching pain of my heart was felt in every part of my body. "I am feeling very ill, Jens. Please take care of Hans and Yern today." I isolated myself in our bunk, covered my head, and slept for days. Sleep was the only place to escape the pain of living. I could not admit to anyone that I was avoiding life by burying myself in the darkness, but I used the opportunity to tell a half-truth, and the results were exactly what I intended.

Jens kept me informed of the ship's status. "Annie. I wished you could have been on deck today because we beheld a spectacular site. The ship sailed between two islands; Jamaica was on our left and Cuba on our right. We were within a mile of Cuba, and we could see palm trees and fields, surrounded by beautiful turquoise waters. It was a site well worth remembering."

Jens told me about the morning meetings, particularly the day President Olsen discussed New Orleans. "President Olsen said many saints do not have passage beyond New Orleans, the final port for the *Benjamin Adams*. Several families will be left there, without the means to buy tickets for the steamship to St Louis and Kansas City. President Olsen said he does not want any person left behind in the 'wicked, swampy city of New Orleans', and for that reason, a donation box has been set up."

"Annie, I want you to know am giving President Olsen enough money to pay for five additional tickets on the steamship. Each adult ticket to St Louis is approximately $3.50 and children are half that amount. While this donation may cut us short, I do not believe this will put us at risk."

"I trust you, Jens. Do what you feel is right." I kept my feelings to myself, burying my body deep in our bed, consumed with thoughts of Mads. I remembered the Christmas season when Mads was born. We all fussed over him. Our new baby, the precious little gift we received for Christmas. We were so hopeful for Mads future; the son born to help heal the loss of our firstborn.

I remembered the time Mads fell down, striking his little chin on a rock. I was surprised at how much blood could come from a small laceration. Jens looked at Mads' s wound and was not impressed with the severity. I insisted Jens hitch up the horse and take Mads to the doctor.

"It is a good thing you brought him in, Jens." The doctor scolded. "The laceration is deep and needs to be stitched together." *I sat quietly, not saying a word. Just be thankful for the doctor's surgical skills, Annie.*

If I closed my eyes I could almost feel the softness of Mads's skin against mine. I could see his smile and feel his fidgety little hands playing with his long brown hair. I wanted to linger with him. I could not seem to let go.

As the days wore on, the steerage became filled with an

increasing number of ill and suffering passengers. It seems that a great number of Danes were made ill by the oppressive climate. They took refuge in their bunks with weakness and misery, too ill to be on the upper deck. For me, there was no escaping my sorrow and intense heartache, no matter the conditions of steerage, no matter the staggering heat.

"Annie. I am very concerned about you." Jens looked into my eyes, searching for the woman he had married. "Perhaps you will not live to see the promised land." The thought had crossed my mind, but hearing Jens utter the words was brutal. I did not respond. I could not respond.

Am I willing to stay in our bed, in my pitiful condition and give up? Am I going to abandon my three remaining children because I had lost Mads? Can I throw away my dreams to live in Zion with Jens?

Sixteen

Think not, when you gather to Zion,
The Saints here have nothing to do
But tend to your personal welfare,
And always be comforting you.
No, Saints who are faithful
Are doing what they find to do, with their might;
To accomplish the gathering of Israel
They're toiling by day and by night.
Eliza R. Snow

"Annie, please, you must drink this broth." Margarethe helped me into a sitting position on the edge of the bunk, watching as I sipped the bitterness. "Annie. I know how you have struggled since you left Denmark. I have never lost a child, so I can only imagine the sorrow of losing two of your children. The Lord has asked so much of you. For that I am sorry; but it is time for you to get out of bed. It is time for you to move on. We have not reached our destination and you cannot quit now."

Margarethe's words were harsh, but I knew her honesty was spoken out of love and concern. I could count on Margarethe to be there for me. Tears filled my eyes. "Yes, Margarethe, you are right. It is time to move on." Supporting my weight with hers, Margarethe helped me up the stairs into the bright healing sunshine. We found a place on the upper deck.

"It is too hot in the direct sun, Annie. Please. Sit over here." Margarethe and I sat in a shaded area, on a sturdy wooden box surrounded by the beautiful turquoise waters of the Gulf of Mexico. The water was calming, and the sunshine, healing.

"Are you feeling well enough to stay here a little longer?"

"Yes, Margarethe. The heat is intense, but being here on the deck feels wonderful."

"Annie, I am curious. Does Jens know where you will live once we arrive in Utah?"

"No. Jens has no idea where we will be going, but he is determined to stake a claim of fertile land; a place he can farm and have a blacksmith shop."

"Lars tells me that Brigham Young will likely direct us to a particular location. We will go where we are directed." Margarethe's faith and confidence were contagious.

"Knowing not where we will be sent makes me anxious, but when Jens talked with missionaries from America, they told him it matters not where we are sent; every community will be full of loving, peaceful saints."

"I remember what our leaders told us." Margarethe smiled. "They said all of Utah is peaceful and quiet with no war. It is a happy and lovely place. They said it is a poet's dream, realized in this life, where we are equally rich, and none are truly poor. They said each person has free access to land for the good of all, without money or price."

I gazed into the azure waters as Margarethe's words soaked into my soul. The vivid image of Utah was revived, for I had forgotten the promise. *Yes, there is a place where peace and equality survive, where the land is most beautiful and the climate is healthy; a place where the saints can dwell and become the richest people on earth!*

"Margarethe, I want you to know how grateful I am to be your friend and sister in the Lord. I treasure the day we met and the friendship we have come to know. When my faith has been shaken to my core, you have been there for me. I have always admired your faith and trust in God to direct your every step. My faith is not so strong. It seems as though the line for me between fear and faith is very narrow."

"Thank you, Annie. I share the same love for you. Please remember, my friend, you are not any different than most people when it comes to faith. Let me remind you of the story of Peter from the Book of Matthew. Peter had great faith, enough to walk on the water as long as he stayed focused on the Lord. But when he let his focus change to the unsettled waters, his fear overpowered his faith and he began to sink."

"Yes, I understand. I have been sinking in the waters for sure."

Margarethe delivered to me a most needed spiritual message. I was filled with thankfulness to God for giving us the Word, our guide, and source of strength. My physical strength slowly returned and the frequent meetings between Margarethe and me became like an ointment on a wound.

"Annie. Did Jens tell you that the ship is almost out of drinking water?"

"No! He did not say anything about water, but he did tell me the ship has been drifting back and forth for the last eight days without making any headway."

"That is true, Annie. Days ago we were made aware that the rations are almost depleted, including the water. President Olsen has asked the strong, healthy people to fast, and everyone to pray for winds. We need winds to take us to the mouth of the Mississippi River before we die from starvation or thirst. I am sure Jens did not tell you, lest you be further troubled."

Our conversations were not always so serious. "Remember, Annie, when we first left Liverpool, there were two young single women, continually talking with the sailors? The two women stayed on the upper decks, admiring the sailors, until late in the evening? They all ignored ship rules, not wanting to say goodnight. I recently learned that upon arrival in New Orleans, those same two sailors will be leaving the ship to be baptized and married to those two sisters. They will continue with us on the steamer to Kansas City. Can you believe?"

"What a sweet story, Margarethe. I pray Catherine will marry well, but not until after we arrive in the Utah Valley! She just turned sixteen. She is so mature for her age and she will be a very good wife. I have been so blessed to have married a kind man. Jens has always treated me respectfully and he has been such a good provider."

Margarethe and I continued to meet at our favorite location on the deck each day, reminiscing about days long past, and dreams of the future. "I want a new house with at least three rooms. The children are older now and we need a separate bedroom for the children. Jens tells me the first thing he will purchase is a cooking stove. Oh, Margarethe, I can almost taste freshly baked bread with sweet butter oozing over the crust."

"I agree. I love bread, too, but I have been dreaming of boiled potatoes and creamy gravy; of purple, spicy cabbage and pickled herring. I would give anything to have even one small portion of herring right now. I remember how I spent hours making cookies for our family, and how the sweet treats were gone in minutes. Lefse! Oh, how I love lefse; covered with sweet butter and sugar. Rosettes! Did you ever make rosettes, Annie?"

"Yes, I did, a few times, but I prefer a dessert with some substance, like berry pie!"

Margarethe turned towards me, our eyes met briefly, and simultaneously we broke into laughter. Just when I thought we had finished our silliness, our eyes met again and the laughter started all over. "You are not making our lack of food and water any easier, Margarethe!"

Morning prayer meeting gave us every reason to be hopeful. The captain joined our meeting briefly, thanking everyone for cooperation in rationing of supplies. He indicated we had perhaps two more days of water and rations, and he thought the great "father of waters," the Mississippi River, was about two days away. "Be hopeful, my comrades, we shall soon see land."

The sea changed colors, from a silky blue to a muddy yellow and emigrants began gathering on deck, hopeful to get the first glimpse of land. It was the very next day, late in the afternoon on March 19, when I heard shouting from a watchful shipmate. "There! Over there! I see a lighthouse!" The news moved through the crowd of emigrants like a wave of the sea, erupting into a deafening shout of joy. *Me thinks all of heaven must have heard the jubilation.*

The captain hoisted the pilot-flag and soon a river pilot came on board, taking us closer to the river's mouth where we anchored. Very few of us slept that night. How could we? Our blood was drenched in anticipation of landing, for it had been six weeks and three days since we had been towed out of Liverpool.

Seventeen

Think not, when you gather to Zion,
The prize and the victory is won.
Think not that the warfare is ended,
The work of salvation is done.
No, no; for the great Prince of Darkness
A ten-fold exertion will make
When he sees you approaching the fountain
Where truth you may freely partake.
Eliza R Snow

Worn and weary, we climbed from steerage to the deck, making sure the land had not disappeared. It was a glorious morning with wisps of fog and noisy gulls hanging next to the shoreline. Seeing land again brought a mix of feelings. We felt relief, knowing we would not likely starve, nor die from thirst. Relief that we would soon be rid of the Benjamin Adams, a place we called home far too long. We were ecstatic, just thinking of standing on solid ground and touching the soil of America.

Our family stood on deck all day, fascinated by the massive three-storied steamer that took the *Benjamin Adams* and three other sailing ships in tow, heading up the great Mississippi River.

"As far as I can see, it is swampy land. Just swamps filled with trees and reeds."

"I wonder if people live in this area?"

"I do not know where they would live."

"Did you notice all the different lighthouses as we moved up the river? People must be living there."

"I am told the little town of LaBalize is on the starboard."

"Look at that place! Every house is a little structure built on stilts."

"This would be a very difficult place to raise cattle."

"I see a few cattle over there in that small pasture."

All day we feasted on sites and soaked in the sounds, hoping to catch a glimpse of life in America. By dusk, we were drenched from the body-soaking heat and humidity. The crew dropped anchor for the night.

The convoy of ships started very early the next morning, sailing against the tide, past several good harbors. We could see views of sugar plantations, stately mansions ,and groves of orange trees. We could see cows and sheep munching on lush grass, and we enjoyed the wildlife, the birds, and ducks, wild turkeys and wolves.

That night we were an audience to the loudest, most violent thunder and lightning storm I had ever known. Thunder boomed over and over, rolling across the blackened sky. Through the darkest of dark, lightning filled the sky with cracking and snapping of zig-zagging electrified designs. The heavens seemed to be fighting a battle of war, while torrents of rain flooded and pounded the decking.

The next morning our ship continued towards New Orleans. We stood on deck, observing rows of green orchards, and farms lining both sides of the river. We could see black slaves working in the fields, and black children ran to the banks of the river, waving to our ships as we passed. "Did you notice, Annie? There are six black men, working on the steamship. They seem to be doing all the heaviest work."

"Is it true? I was told that black slaves can be bought in New Orleans? All the beauty of this land is diminished in my eyes when I think of black men and women, owned as slaves." Jens silently shook his head in agreement.

Several times our ships ran aground on sandbars, delaying us several hours before we were able to continue. Finally, we reached the harbor of New Orleans in the middle of the afternoon of March 22. There was a mighty celebration of cheering and shouting when the *Benjamin* was finally secured to the docks. Two agents from Zion came aboard to help us. "Welcome to New Orleans. I have good news, all ye people! All is well in Zion. They send their most heartfelt greetings. For your information, we have secured the steamboat, *M. Kennett*, for your passage on to St Louis."

The agents continued. "We have hired wagons to be here early tomorrow morning. Any person wanting to buy items for the journey will be taken to the city and returned to the docks.

"Be careful of your diet. Do not eat fresh vegetables or fruits! The drinking water is not fit for consumption." Warned the agents. "The drinking water for this city is piped directly from the Mississippi River and should be avoided at all cost. The land and water are cursed here."

"Children. Listen to the warnings given by our leaders. Take heed to follow their advice." We resigned ourselves to follow this advice, but too soon we would discover that everyone did not heed the warning.

The Port of New Orleans was situated one hundred miles upriver from the point where the river pilot took control of our ship. The port was on a lowland, about five miles long, with swamps and bogs all around. The port was filled with a thousand sailing ships, mostly three-masted, and a few smaller vessels. Thousands of workers, mostly black slaves, bustled about, loading and unloading the freight.

"Annie, I will take Hans and go to town with the men. When the wagons come back we will move our belongings to the *Kennett*." Jens said. In the afternoon we were allowed to board the new steamship. This ship was built to carry emigrants, and the accommodations were grand. However, our group tickets were "deck passenger tickets." The blacks carried our luggage from one ship to the other, and to my astonishment, they were kind and polite. Even the sailors on the *Kennett* treated us more kindly than we had previously experienced. Without a bed or shelter, we found room among the cargo crates. "Annie, this space will work for us, even if we are not able to spread out." We were so crowded; it seemed like we would be sleeping in an upright position.

"Annie, when we went to the New Orleans market we saw a public business of slave trading. I saw black men, tall and well-built, being auctioned for 400-500 dollars each. There were women and children, sold like chattel. It was excruciating to watch this business. I was told New Orleans is the only city in this state where slaves can be bought and sold. The slave trade is a big business, because merchants and wealthy families keep slaves, men as well as women.

"You should have seen the market," Jens explained. "The market was held in two long wooden structures, open only for foot traffic, and filled with people; kind, friendly people. There was meat, milk, grain and fresh vegetables brought daily to the market and offered at cheap prices. I found powdered sugar at four cents a pound. Rice was just one cent a pound, and butter only 12 1/2 cents a pound! While groceries are cheap, other items were very expensive, like the boots I saw for myself that were 16 dollars.

"The streets were wide and straight, but muddy, dirty and smelly. I saw a dead cow laying in the street! Conditions are quite unsanitary, Annie. We rode past a new four-story building, still under construction with walls of granite, a rather imposing site. It is to be the new Customs House. We saw the Hotel Charles, a beautiful four-story building and other new buildings under construction, but nothing could compare to the size and expense of the Customs House."

Late in the afternoon on March 25, the *Kennett* pulled away from the pier, heading up the Mississippi River. The river was of immense width, filled with winter; dirty with mud and ice that came from miles away. No one could have guessed as to the number and variety of vessels that filled the waters. The *Kennett*, like the other steamships working the Mississippi, was nearly flat-bottomed and quite capable of maneuvering the shallow water.

Jens and I stood together on the crowded deck, delighted with the beauty of the landscape. Sugar plantations and blooming orange groves were gorgeous. Forests of cottonwood trees and meadows lined both sides of the river. I felt rejuvenated. "Do not worry another minute about me, Jens. Getting off the *Benjamin*, enjoying a good meal, being on land, and starting this leg of our journey has brought me the much-needed strength I needed."

Firmly stuck on a sandbar, the Kennett became grounded during the first night. Grinding engines and shouting sailors woke us during the excitement. It took hours for the captain to break loose the ship before we could move on. When the skies warmed with daylight we received the dreadful news of an unwelcome guest on our ship. Cholera! The warnings given in New Orleans had not been sufficient to deter starving passengers. During the first night, many passengers became dreadfully sick.

Cholera outbreaks were deadly, and the very whisper of the word caused the crew and passengers to panic. Fear of disease, especially cholera, was the very reason we went to such lengths on the *Benjamin Adams* to keep the ship and the people clean. Although a specific cause of the disease was unknown, nor was it known how it was transmitted, there were certain measures we took to avoid the disease. We knew once cholera was contracted the results were almost immediate, with intestinal cramping and diarrhea, vomiting and dehydration and most certainly death within one or two days. In the confines of the steamship, an epidemic was likely, which meant isolation and quarantine for a vessel for at least 30 days.

Maren Neilsen, from Middlefart, Denmark, was the first to exhibit symptoms. She became ill during the night, vomiting and screaming with pain. Nothing could be done, and Maren died the next morning. Three additional people were dead by the following day, March 27. The ship's carpenter made simple boxes for the emigrants and just before dark, the ship pulled to land, where the bodies were carried a short distance into the woods and buried.

"Jens, I do not understand. How is it possible to have come this far, suffer through the challenges of the sea, only to find our family in the middle of this beautiful Mississippi River Valley, subject to an outbreak of cholera? What can we do?" The options were few.

Gathering our children, Jens held a conference. "Catherine, Hans, and Yern. Listen carefully. Several of our friends are suffering from Cholera. I need to make sure you understand our new rules. You are not to drink the ship's water, not for any reason. You should not even wash your hands in the water."

Our family tried to isolate ourselves as space would allow, eating only the food that Jens had bought in New Orleans and drinking only hot coffee or tea purchased from the ship's kitchen. We watched as the country became more mountainous and as far as the eye could see, the land was thick with woods. The river current was powerful, pushing against the banks, often causing them to collapse. Without soil, tree roots were exposed, and the trees fell victim to the river. With each fallen tree, the river was made wider, though not deeper, and river traffic became more treacherous.

The ship made a stop at a picturesque settlement built on a hillside, with a small church perched on the edge of the highest peak. The *Kennett* stopped briefly, just long enough to take on wood for fuel and to bury two additional saints that had died during the night. We were not allowed to get off the ship.

The voyage up the Mississippi to St Louis, a distance of 1300 miles usually took six to eight days, but our travel took ten days in total. Evenings were often filled with fierce thunderstorms, and we became accustomed to the *Kennett* being stuck on sandbars. "What is wrong now? Are we stuck on another sandbar?" Hans inquired.

"Not a sand bar, Hans. They say the ship ran against a tree trunk, damaging the hull and destroying much freight." The river was a continuous obstacle course.

We were most thankful this accident happened during the daylight, for if it had been night, the results could have been much different. It was several hours before the ship was repaired and we could continue.

We huddled amongst the cargo while intense thunder and lightning storms pounded around us and the captain maneuvered our ship past sunken steamers and floating debris. We passed small villages with strange names like Nidshid, Quickbonne, and Napolean. The *Kennett* moored, but for a short time, at the mountain city of Memphis. We could not go ashore. We moored for the night at Caira, a city built where the Ohio River flows into the Mississippi. We passed remains of steamships, still visible in the river, having met their demise from floating ice or boiler eruptions, but cholera panic was the greatest obstacle that ruled our days on the river.

We met in small groups, not formal prayer meetings, and gathered to pray for the sick. We prayed for those families that were personally touched by death. The disease crept through the cargo area, down hallways, and through berths, attacking both young and old, the defenseless and the undernourished. More than one-half of our people lay sick and vomiting. "Oh, God, have mercy on us. Protect us from the dreadful disease now haunting this ship."

Eighteen

$\mathcal{F}$illed with sick and dying, the steamer pressed on towards St. Louis. President Olsen appointed several men, including Jens, to visit every family twice a day, ministering to the sick. Jens was busy with the brethren, assisting where possible, while I stayed close to our family and belongings.

Jens explained. "Annie, we prayed with a sister, and as long as she could swallow I gave her sips of wine, diluted with sugar and water. Still, after everything we did, the sister died. We tried to console her husband and young daughter, grieving the death of their wife and mother, but I am afraid we did not make much difference. I struggled to hold back my emotions.

"I heard an unpleasant conversation between President Olsen and the captain of the *Kennett*." Jens continued. "I could not understand what they were saying, but the captain was shouting and jabbing his finger on President Olsen's chest. I later learned what the captain had said.

"The captain told President Olsen our people had been warned time after time to be careful of exposing themselves to disease in New Orleans. Yet, when we landed, the emigrants started eating fresh meat and vegetables and drinking the 'stinking water.' Now we have a ship full of 'chollery' which could have been avoided if counsel had been obeyed."

"What was President Olsen's response?"

"There was little he could say. He knew the captain was speaking the truth."

"Jens, have you seen Margarethe and Brother Lars? How are they doing?"

"Margarethe and Lars seem to be just fine, but that does not mean much, Annie. Cholera sneaks up on a person so quickly. Margarethe could seem quite fine in the morning, but she could take ill tonight and be dead before the next sunset. This disease is deadly.

"I have located John Munsen, the young man that came with us from Vejle. We are his only family, so I have been checking on him at least twice a day. I have seen Jens and Karen Nielsen, our friends from Bornholm. They all seem to be strong and healthy, including their new baby.

"Annie, depression and sorrow pervade the ship. Every hour more people take sick and die. The death count has now reached fourteen, and we have one more day before we reach St. Louis.

"You might be interested in what I learned today." Jens continued. "In the year of 1832, St Louis lost several hundred of their citizens from a cholera epidemic. Cholera abruptly ended, only to return with vengeance in December 1848. Cholera decimated emigrants as well as prominent citizens and in six months over 4,600 people had died from the disease. Some blamed the epidemic on a local newspaper that had begun publishing on Sunday, and others blamed the German's sauerkraut! Most believe, however, that cholera is a result of a thick cloud of death hanging in the air, forming toxic gases from rotting vegetation and human waste.

"They thought Cholera was a result of bad sauerkraut?

That is ridiculous." I was amused at the thought. "If that were the case, most of the Germans would be dead by now."

"I am more surprised that the religious zealots thought it was a result of men working on the Sabbath."

"In the spring of 1849 St Louis took over Arsenal Island and renamed it Quarantine Island." Jens explained. "The new law requires all ships must stop there to be inspected. Any person showing symptoms of a disease must remain where the ill are nursed, in a hospital built on the island, until they recover or die. The victims are not allowed off the island, but are buried in a graveyard near the hospital."

"Jens, be so careful. I know you need to help the sick, but please, be wise and stay healthy. We need you."

Shortly after noon on April 1, 1854, we arrived at Quarantine Island. I was feeling well, as were our children, so there was no reason to be anxious or think our family would be detained. I noticed, however, just before we landed, many of the sick had disappeared. *That is strange, I thought. Where did they go?* The inspection began, if that is what one would call it, and then I understood. Most of the ill had hidden in the women's lounge. As the physician came around, he greeted the women nearby. "Good afternoon, ladies." The physician continued with his rounds, passing by the restroom without any further inquiry as to who might be inside.

"Annie. Hurry. You must come with me." Jens grabbed my hand. "Dorothea Powelson is ill. You must come quickly if you want to see her before she is taken from the ship."

I knew immediately what Jens meant. "Catherine, you are in charge of the boys, until we return " I held on to Jens as we maneuvered through mounds of freight and a maze of people, to the opposite side of the steamship. Tucked in amongst cargo, Dorothea had sought refuge, laying on boards in a makeshift bed of blankets. The moment I saw her, I knew Dorothea was critical.

Her husband, Mads, tried to explain. "Annie. We tried everything we could think of, and we gave her a blessing. The doctor examined her and says she is ill with cholera. That means Dorothea must be taken to the island hospital. The children and I will stay with her until she is well."

It was heart-breaking to say goodbye to Dorothea. I tried to speak with optimism but nearly choked on my words. I knew it would be a miracle if we saw her again. "Dorothea." I took her hand. "The doctors will take care of you. We will see you soon, in Kansas City, when you are well again. I'll be praying for you, my friend."

The *Kennett* continued the four miles into the port area of St Louis, "Gateway to the West" arriving late in the afternoon. The critically ill had been left behind, and now the *Kennett* would be put in quarantine. Passengers were allowed to sleep on the *Kennett* one more night, and we chose to remain with the group rather than sleep on the docks.

Our early morning prayer meeting brought much-needed news. "Brethren. We have secured a steamship that will depart tomorrow, as soon as our freight is loaded. You are individually responsible for transferring your personal items and luggage to the steamer, *Australia*. If you plan to make your wagon purchase in Kansas City, we urge you to instead make that purchase here in St. Louis. Wagon supplies are nearly depleted in Kansas City. We have also made arrangements for those who desire to purchase additional provisions to be taken into town before the *Australia* departs."

The excitement was invigorating as we moved off the *Kennett*. One by one the families pulled and dragged their lives down the bustling pier. We moved in and around huge piles of freight cluttering the wharf, about one-half mile to the steamship, *Australia*. The *Australia* was at least 250 feet long with a 40-foot beam and had accommodations for over 400 people and 500 tons of freight. This would be the final leg of our water travel, another 350 miles on the Missouri River.

Many of the emigrants did make their wagon purchase in St Louis, as recommended. "Fader, are you going to buy a wagon for us?" Hans inquired.

"Not here, Hans. The wagon was included as a part of our payment I made in Denmark. We were told that our wagon would be supplied in Kansas City, so there is no need to worry about having a wagon."

Loading the freight and wagons on to the third deck took hours longer than anticipated. Passengers boarded and found their quarters, but others preferred sleeping in their wagons during the trip up the Missouri River.

"Come with me." Jens motioned us to follow him. "We need to find a room unless we want to sleep in the cargo area. We may need to share a room with another family."

"I want to sleep with my friends in their wagon." Hans insisted.

"We can put our trunk and loose items here for now." Jens found an empty room and spread out our blanket on the bed. He pushed our trunk into a corner. "Annie, I am taking Hans with me. We will go into town and purchase supplies for the remainder of this trip."

Confident that our only possessions were safe in the small cabin, Catherine, Yern and I set out to explore the floating palace. I had never before seen such lavish furnishings. Nothing was more beautiful than the piano lounge, draped with crimson draperies and matching carpeting.

"Greetings to you Annie." Margarethe smiled. "Have you settled your family in a cabin?"

"Yes, thank you. We are doing just fine. Jens has gone to town to buy some additional supplies."

"You will be just as surprised as I was when I tell you we saw Christian J. and his wife! They found us right after we moored. He looks so good and healthy! It seems like years since we stood on the pier in Copenhagen and waved good-bye to him and the group of saints he is called to lead. Christian J. told me their group came across the Atlantic in the *Jesse Munn* and arrived here in St Louis about seven weeks ago. They have been unable to go further up the river because of ice, so they have sheltered in two different hotels. They have made arrangements to follow us in about a week."

"Thank God for his tender mercies. You must be so proud of your son." I smiled.

My joy was short-lived, however. Our family sat on our bed, in the small cabin of the ship, surrounded by the rewards from Jens's shopping. As we ate fresh bakery bread covered with butter, cheese, and salami, our feast was interrupted with a sharp tapping at the door.

"Annie? Annie, are you there?" I recognized Margarethe's voice.

"Please come in, Margarethe."

"Jens. Annie. I need your help." Margarethe paused, swallowed her emotions and began. "It is Dorothea Powelson's family. I am so sorry to tell you our friend, Dorothea, passed away shortly after she was taken to the hospital. Mads has just returned to the ship with his children. They are all distraught and starving. Please come with me and bring any food that you can spare, some of your bread and cheese will do. Hurry."

We found the Powelson family huddled together, physically and emotionally lost. Mads was surrounded by his six children, outwardly grieving for their mother. There was Mary, the oldest, holding Soren, her two-year-old baby brother. Annie, a fourteen-year-old, held on to Ane, her five-year-old sister and Mikkel and Paul clung to their father's arms.

Jens embraced Mads. "I am so sorry for your loss, my friend. What can we do to help? We have brought food for you and your family, please eat."

Dorothea was gone, leaving Mads with the responsibility of completing the journey and raising their six children on his own. I felt a great loss, but I am sure my loss was nothing compared to the loss felt by these children. We Saints were accustomed to supporting and strengthening families during times of sorrow, so as we had done before, our people embraced Mads's family, helping to care for the children and trying to make less their grief.

Nineteen

*T*he scene from the *Australia* was spectacular. Thousands of dockworkers scurried about like ants, working to load and unload freight. Long wagons, drawn by horses, waited in lines to unload and reload their cargo. Hundreds of ships came and went, belching steam into the Missouri sky, and a small band played festive music on the pier. I stopped to enjoy the distinct sound of a fast-picking banjo. It was late in the afternoon of April 5 when the Australia loosed it's mooring and began moving up the Mississippi River.

In the middle of the night, we reached the confluence of the Missouri and Mississippi Rivers. The captain called the Missouri " a most cantankerous river" because the river's obstacles were just as threatening or worse than the Mississippi. We passed by dense forests and mountains, past small towns with strange names like Augusta, Hermann, and Shitubert. We passed the capital of Missouri, Jefferson City, and moored in a small city of Nahsoun for the night.

Jens tossed and turned, making it impossible for me to sleep. "Is something wrong, Jens?" I whispered, so as not to wake the children. "Annie. I am feeling quite miserable. I will get up and go for a walk. Perhaps that will help."

Jens was gone quite awhile before returning to our cabin. We were all awake when he returned. "Annie. I need to lay down. My stomach is cramping and I am sick with nausea."

"Oh, Lord, please. Not cholera!" I helped Jens get onto the bed. "Catherine, would you go find Brother Lars and Margarethe. Ask them to come quickly."

We did everything we could think of to help Jens. Brother Larsen and Brother Nielsen gave him a priesthood blessing. Margarethe, bless her soul, took our children with her to allow Jens the privacy he needed. Throughout the day, she came to give me encouragement and advice as I cared for Jens. "Annie, please make sure that Jens drinks the wine I brought. I have diluted the wine with clean water."

Watching Jens writhe in pain was exhausting both physically and emotionally. "Please, Jens. You must drink of the wine that we have prepared." The day dragged on as the *Australia* maneuvered the river, all the while, Jens's condition seemed to worsen. I felt totally helpless. I covered Jens's head with a cool damp cloth and I stroked his arm. "Jens." My voice was one of pleading. "You must fight this battle. Your family needs you. I need you. Take us to Zion, Jens."

Panic crept up my spine, fear filled my head and tears ran down my face. I turned away, hoping that Jens would not notice. *What would I do without him? I could not comprehend my life without Jens. Oh, God! You have brought us this far and tested our resolve almost more than I can endure. I can not go on without Jens. Oh, God, hear my prayer. Heal him.*

"Annie," Jens spoke slowly and barely audible. "I love you. I have loved you from the day I first saw you in Gauerslund Church." He paused as pulsing pain swept over his body.

"I understand, Jens. Lay still and save your energy."

Jens was determined to continue. "I tried to provide." His speech was slow, his breathing more shallow. "I love our family, Annie. Our children...I am so proud."

Yes, Jens. I understand. I believe I understand how proud you are of our children. I see it in your eyes. I am so thankful for our family, too. We are truly blessed with good children. You have been such a great provider for our family."

"Annie, if I die," Jens hesitated, "you must promise me you will carry on." Silence filled the room. I held my breath, unable to answer. Jens found the strength to continue. "Annie, be strong. Take our family to Zion. You must live our dream."

"What dream?" My voice quivered with emotion. "I am not sure I can even remember our dream. I can barely remember why you sold our home and why we left the land we loved. I can not remember. Why are we here in this disease infested land and two of our children lay buried behind us? Tell me why, Jens?"

"I am sorry, Annie." Jens cried. I tried to wipe Jens's brow, but he pushed away my attempts. He raised from the pillow slightly, and took a deep breath before he began again. "The first time I brought the missionaries for dinner," Jens' spoke with shortness of breath, "you were unhappy. Remember? You changed when you heard Brother Lauritz preach."

"Yes, Jens, I remember how very unhappy I was with you. I wanted to hear none of the Mormon messages. But, I still recall the powerful feeling that came over me that day when the missionaries prayed and started preaching. Without a doubt, I knew those two young men were sent by God. They spoke inspired words of truth."

"Annie, remember. We have been called to Zion because of the truth."

"Yes, Jens." My eyes looked into his. 'Yes, I remember."

I tried to help Jens, but there was nothing more I could do. He continued to worsen, wreathing in pain and before nightfall I was feeling quite ill myself. I tried to ignore the initial symptoms, thinking it impossible that I, too, might have cholera. Just as the evening arrived, and the ship moored for the night, I could no longer ignore the fact that I was very ill. "Oh Lord, have you forgotten about us? Have we traveled all this way only to perish for nothing?"

Our situation was critical, and I knew it. Now that I have filled with nausea myself, I was not able to help Jens. "Oh, Jens. I'm so sorry. What are we to do?" I cried to the heavens. "Please God. Have mercy on us."

Margarethe knew as soon as she opened our cabin door. "Lars, we must find another Elder to pray for Annie. She is quite ill. The very air in this cabin is saturated with cholera."

Margarethe touched me, gently stroking my feverish body. "Annie, we came to check on the two of you before we retired for the evening. You need to drink more liquids." I stirred from my sleep.

"Jens. Wake, my brother. Wake up. You need to have another drink." Brother Lars attempted to stir Jens with a more forceful command. "Wake, brother Jens. I am here to help you."

The silence was deafening. I felt the urgency of Brother Lars' voice as he tried several times to stir Jens. Then I heard three bone-chilling words uttered by Brother Lars that filled the poisoned air of our room. "Jens is gone, Margarethe. Please stay with Annie. I will go find President Olsen."

"Margarethe?" I reached for the hand of my dear friend. "Margarethe. Tell me it is not so? Jens is gone? He can not be gone. This is not possible." I looked into Margarethe's eyes, pleading for an answer contradicting the words I had so clearly heard. "Say it is not so."

"Annie, I am so sorry." Margarethe's voice was filled with emotion. "It is true. Jens has left us."

Grief filled every part of my being and I forgot all reason to breathe. I cried out to the heavens with every ounce of strength I had within me. "Take me with you, Jens. I can not go on living without you."

"Be still, my friend. Be still." Margarethe wiped my face. "You are very sick. Annie, you must find every ounce of strength you have to fight this disease. Lars and I will be here to help you, but your little family needs you now more than ever."

"Annie." Margarethe held my hand. "The brethren are here to take Jens' body." Brother Lars wrapped Jens in a soft woolen blanket, while another brother offered a brief prayer. Together the brethren lifted my dear husband from the bed and removed his body from our room.

"Lars, I must stay with Annie. Would you please go fetch her children?"

Brother Lars woke Catherine, Hans, and Yern from their sleeping. I dare not imagine their reaction when Brother Lars told them of their father's passing. When they arrived in my room, they clung together at the side of my bed, sobbing and crying. Margarethe tried to comfort them as best she could.

My children were lost in the depths of grief and devastation. They were filled with fear. I recognized those feelings because I felt the same. I had lost my will to live, but I realized that somehow I had forgotten our children. I had forgotten that our children were filled with the fear of losing both parents. "Your mother is very ill, children." Margarethe tried to comfort, but her arms were not sufficient to comfort us all.

Catherine threw her body down on the bed next to me and cried. "Mother, I shall not go on without you. I will not be left an orphan. I am going to stay with you until I get the dreadful disease."

Hans and Yern held on to Margarethe, crying softly as they listened to Catherine's dramatic display. "Mother., Hans spoke aloud. "Mother, I will say a prayer for you."

At daylight, before the ship left its moorings, Jens's body was buried without a casket at water's edge, among the reeds of the Missouri River. The burial was done quickly and quietly, without the presence of any family or friends. I lay in bed so ill I could barely lift my head. The thought of Jens's body lying in the thick mud without a marker, without a proper burial, haunted me forever.

"Oh, God. I need thee. Where is your solace?"

Twenty

*L*ate in the afternoon of April 10, the *Austrailia* moored at Westport, our final destination on the river. Our arrival was absent from cheering or celebration, for all the saints were weary and a great many were ill. This city was small, approximately six miles from the City of Kansas, and a short distance from the Missouri River. This would be the outfitting place for the saints who were crossing the plains.

Our small family was not left wanting. "Annie, just lean on me." Margarethe held me by my arm. "I will help you down the plank and on to the dock. Brother Lars will help your children and we have brought Brother John Munsen to help with your trunk and personal belongings."

The Danish Saints, what remained of them, disembarked from the *Australia*. Weary from travel, and ill with cholera, they dragged their only possessions off the ship and deposited them in the sand. Even though I was very ill, I could sense an attitude of gratitude among the saints, for we believed that the hardest part of our travels was behind us!

President Olsen stood in the mix, guiding and directing the saints. "Brethren, for safety reasons, it would be best to travel to our camp in small family groups. It is just a short distance to walk, about a mile. We will remain there until our company is outfitted. For those of you who have made the purchase of your wagons in St. Louis, please walk to

our camp. Use your wagons to transport the ill, instead."
Thanks to the kindness of other saints, I did not have to
walk. Even still, riding in a wagon for a mile, for someone as
ill as I, seemed mighty far.

Our camp was located in a forest where an open space
allowed for hundreds of tents to be raised. As far as the eye
could see, there were rows of tents filled with thousands
of Scandinavian emigrants. The wagons purchased in St.
Louis became adequate sleeping quarters for some. Huts of
shrubs became the shelter for others until tents could be
erected. Thank God for John Munsen and other brethren
who raised a tent for our family. They made sure that we
had a safe, dry place to sleep and clean water before they
found their own shelter.

Exhausted beyond imagination, filled with cholera, and
wracked with sorrow, I laid my body down on a makeshift
bed of homemade quilts. I fell into a deep sleep.

I dreamed of Jens. I could see his eyes. He was not ill. I
felt his presence, and he spoke clearly. "Annie, do not worry. You are an elect woman. Your emigration to Zion has
a great and mighty purpose. Be at peace. God has brought
you this far, Annie. He is with you."

Jens' voice was so close and clear that I was startled awake.
"Jens?" I spoke his name aloud. "Jens, where are you?"

"Moder, Moder. You must be dreaming. Please take another drink of broth." Catherine tried to console me. I lay
still, pondering the dream and remembering the voice. I
knew Jens's voice and it was so clearly his voice. Jens had
brought a personal message, a priceless gift for me. The
dream was monumental because from that moment on I

drew on the promise from Jens. God was with me, and I knew it. I was filled with an intense desire to live. I was filled with faith that with God's strength, I could carry on. *I will fight this disease. God willing, I will not be another victim of cholera. Besides, I can think of at least three important reasons to gather my resolve and press on. Those reasons are named Catherine, Hans, and Yern.*

The blackness of night and the darkness of cholera continued to fill our camp. Unfamiliar sounds of chattering night critters filled the air, but it was the moaning from Catherine that convinced me she was now ill with cholera. I thought perhaps Hans and Yern would escape the illness, but before the day was over they were also overcome with nausea and intestinal cramping. A great number of the camp not only contracted cholera but measles as well. I never knew how many died, but I knew that the great number of ill put a burden on the healthy ones, who cared for those who could not care for themselves.

My family was among those who received countless hours of selfless service from our fellow saints. Margarethe and Brother Lars lovingly watched over us, bringing fresh water and broth for our family. John Munson was there, too, inspecting our tent and building a fire pit. There was little I could do but sleep. Despite our conditions, in the silence of my confines, I kept my resolve. I would be healthy again.

"Wake up, Catherine. Wake up, boys. Are you all feeling a little better today?" Margarethe's voice filled the tent. "Annie, let us try to get the Jasperson family out for a little walk today."

"I think that is a wonderful idea." I sat up slightly on my elbow. With Margarethe's help, I was able to stand, take a few steps from the stuffy tent and join the living. "How many days have we been here?"

"We have been in Westport over a week now, and cholera continues to claim more lives of our people. Your friend, Karen Neilsen, lost her only baby a few days ago. Several of the saints gathered for a brief memorial, and Karen's little girl was buried in the field on the edge of our camp."

"I understand what Karen is feeling. She and her husband must be heartbroken right now."

"Annie, I know how difficult these past days have been for you. I have been helping so many families in our company and there are only a few that have escaped the pain of losing a family member. However, in the midst of great sorrow, I have seen God's hand holding us, as He promised. President Olsen read a scripture at the burial for Karen's baby that was very comforting. God promised '..for I will go before your face. I will be on your right hand and on your left, and my Spirit shall be in your hearts and mine angels round about you to bear you up'."

I nodded my head in agreement. "That is a beautiful promise, Margarethe. I can tell you I have personally felt the presence of angels round about me since Jens passed away. You know, Margaret, I miss him every minute of the day."

"I can only imagine what life would be like without Brother Lars. Life takes on a new meaning when you lose your mate and partner, your guide, and family's provider."

Margarethe continued. "Annie, your friends, as well as the angels, will hold you up. They will make it possible for you to see Zion. I believe you will not only reach the Utah Valley with your family, but you will prosper there. Generations to come will know your name, and you will be known for your courage and tenacity, in spite of all the obstacles you have known."

The days turned warm with spring. The grove of tall timber surrounding our camp budded out into a canopy of lime green. Wildflowers, strawberries, and grapevines brought signs of new beginnings. Cholera gradually lost the powerful grip on our family, allowing us to return to the tasks of daily life in the camp. Every day Hans would ask me. "When are we going to get our wagon? When do we get our oxen? Are we ever going to leave this place?" We waited, and grew tired of waiting. Where were the wagons and oxen?

One evening, as we sat around the campfire, John explained some of the reasons for the delay. "Brother Olsen told us that the frontier agent, William Empey, is finding it almost impossible to locate livestock. Cattle are both scarce and costly. Since the gold discovery in California in the year 1848, thousands of hungry miners have driven up the price of livestock. Eastern businessmen bought all the cattle, horses and sheep they could find. They herded them by the tens of thousands to the markets of the West for incredible prices and enormous profits. Locally, the prices have increased drastically even as compared to last season."

The saints, led by Christian J., arrived in the Westport Camp on May ninth. Winter had forced their company to wait in St. Louis, where their critically ill had passed away. By the time their company arrived in Westport, they were a healthier group. There was every reason to celebrate and give thanks when our companies were combined and new leadership was formed. Our own President Olsen was called to be the leader of the combined companies and we would be forever known as the Hans Peter Olsen Company. No one was more pleased than Margarethe, for now, their family was nearly complete. Only Margarethe's youngest son, Lauritz, remained in Denmark.

Margarethe and I sat on a makeshift bench next to our campfire, visiting in the cool of the evening. "Christian J. called for a company-wide prayer meeting, a gathering of celebration and thanks to God for delivering us this far. President Olsen forbid the meeting."

"Why would President Olsen refuse his request for a prayer meeting?"

"He told Christian J. that we are in hostile territory and our lives are at risk while we are camping here in Westport. Many Mormons have suffered persecution here. They have even been murdered in their homes.

"An order for the extermination of Mormons, issued by Governor Boggs of Missouri, still exists today. For that reason, we have armed guards posted night and day around our camp. Although recent reports of violence are few, no leader would take unnecessary risks by worshiping in an assembly."

"Yes," I responded, "I remember how saints were persecuted in Denmark, but I was not aware of what you call 'extermination orders' for the saints in Missouri."

Sunday, May 28, was a beautiful glorious morning without a cloud in the sky. We held our first worship service since we had arrived at the Westport Camp. Under the security of armed guards, our voices filled the air, singing praises to God. We gathered together in the forenoon, the afternoon, and evening, observing the day in fast. We partook of the sacrament and gloried in the preaching. We filled our souls with the Word, renewing our hope and courage. President Olsen spoke so eloquently. "How is it that we can thank God when we are burdened with sorrow? I suggest that you must set aside your bitterness and fill your heart with gratitude to find healing, peace, and understanding. Thank the Lord, our God, in all things, for that is the only way to find true joy and happiness."

Twenty-One

Our camp, on the very edge of the flowering prairie, was filled with oak trees, wild grapes, and poison oak. We were in our temporary camp so long that it started feeling like "home." With each passing steamship, more saints arrived, swelling the camp population in excess of 1200 emigrants, mostly Danish. The Olson Company, about 550 strong, operated independently from the larger group.

A company meeting was called by President Olson, announcing the organization of smaller, more manageable units. "Our leadership has been called as follows: Brother Christian J. is called as company chaplain, Brother Bent Nielsen as wagon master, Brother Jens Hansen is called to be camp captain, and Brother Peter Thompsen will be captain of the guard.

"When we are totally outfitted, we anticipate having 70 wagons. Each wagon will be outfitted with two yokes of oxen and two cows. We will separate into divisions with approximately 100 people and 10 to 12 wagons. Each division will have a captain. Every wagon family will have a total of 10 to 12 individuals. Since many families are smaller, you may be asked to combine with another family, due to the shortage of wagons.

"Brothers and Sisters, we remain diligent in our efforts to locate the needed livestock, wagons and supplies. We have been delayed far too long here in Westport, and will soon be relocating to a different campsite just a few miles from this location. We must be on the trail before mid-June or we could be stranded in snow before we get into the Utah Valley."

Once we were relocated to our new campsite, we began following the organizational plan, as President Olson outlined. Wagons were assigned to families and food rations distributed. Most of the wagons in our company were reinforced farm wagons, a smaller version of the "prairie schooner." They were about ten feet long, three and one-half feet wide with side rails about three feet high. With its "tongue and neck yoke" attached, the wagon length doubled to about 23 feet and the height was about ten feet tall, with the addition of the "bonnet."

The bonnet was a light brown waterproofed fabric, doubled and stretched over five or six arched wooden bows. This created a cylindrical cover which could be closed at each end. The wagon wheels were different sizes with the rear wheel being about 50 inches in diameter and the front wheel about 44 inches in diameter. The iron tires had wide wooden rims to keep the wagon from sinking into the soft ground. The bottom of the wagon was calked with tar which helped the wagon float when we crossed rivers and protected the wagon contents when we traveled.

Each wagon was given a limit of 2,500 pounds of luggage and provisions. Our rations included: 600 pounds flour, 50 pounds sugar, 50 pounds bacon, 50 pounds rice, 30 pounds beans, 20 pounds dried apples and peaches, five pounds of tea, one-gallon vinegar, 25 pounds salt and ten bars of soap.

John stacked our provisions, stored in bags and crates, into our wagon. "I will be forever indebted to Jens." John spoke with sincerity. "While we have been waiting these past weeks, many of the families find themselves without the necessary funds to be fully outfitted. The shortage of wagons and the added expense for cattle has created an additional burden on many families. Some of our men have been able to find work in local businesses at Westport, or the City of Kansas, while others have not. Many families are thanking Brother Nielsen and Brother Thomsen for their generous contributions, making certain that even though they are not fully outfitted, none are left in the States through lack of money.

"Jens had great foresight when he prepaid for your family, including me, to be fully outfitted. We may not have a coin in our pockets, Annie, but we will not be left behind here in Missouri."

"Yes, John. Jens was a wise businessman, as well as a good father. I miss him every day. Please know how thankful I am for your kindness, and your willingness to be in charge of our oxen and cows. Without you, I am not sure I could manage. Tell me, John. Is it correct that every man from 16 to 60 years of age will be expected to take turns on guard duty, armed and ready to defend our people?"

"Yes, Annie. Even though I just turned 18, I will be assigned guard duty, along with the rest of the men. I have never owned a rifle, so I am not sure what I would do if I had to shoot, particularly at a person."

"I am certain with a little practice you can learn how to shoot a rifle. Wait here. I will be back in a moment, John."

With resolve in my steps, I opened the tent and retrieved one of the hand-made leather scabbards that Jens had carried over his shoulder from our homeland. Jens owned two rifles. There was a shorter double-barrel percussion shotgun and a musket that he had purchased after the Schleswig-Holstein war. I lifted the scabbard holding the heavy musket. Without warning, a rush of salty tears spilled down my face. *Jens's hands will never again hold this musket.*

Brushing aside my emotion, I gathered my composure and carried the scabbard outside the tent. "John, I think Jens would want you to use this. I know very little about rifles, but perhaps one of the brethren would teach you. If you knew how to use it safely, I would feel much safer."

John's eyes grew wide as he pulled the musket from the scabbard and softly rubbed his hands down the barrel. "Sis-sis-ter Jas-Jasperson." John stuttered. "Sis-sis-ter Jasperson, this ri-ri-fle is a-a-mazing. I will...I will find a man to teach me how to shoot."

Unknown until now, an enemy moved into our camp, determined to make miserable our nights. Mosquitoes! The innocent looking bloodthirsty bugs filled our camp and tents, relentless in their pestering, causing great welts over much of our bodies. Mosquitoes were not the only reason our sleeping was disturbed. We experienced fierce storms of thunder, booming, rolling and clapping as it moved across the prairie. Cowering in the blackness of our tents, unable to actually see the bolts of lightning, we could feel the electricity in the dusty, humid air. Drenching rain pounded down, and fierce swirling winds threatened to blow away our fragile shelters, with the frightened occupants inside.

The storm continued throughout the night and most of the next day, but there was little we could do. We remained inside the tent, without hot food or drinks until the next evening.

"You must be Sister Jasperson. I am not certain we have met, but I am Brother Carl Capson. I knew Jens. He was a great man. I am so sorry for your loss." Brother Capson continued. "I have been called as one of the division captains, and your family has been assigned under my supervision for the remainder of the journey.

"I understand that John Munson, as well as other saints, helped set up your tent. I was told they nurtured you and your children through your illness and back to good health. I also understand your wagon is loaded with your supplies. Our oxen and cows will soon arrive, allowing our company to start the journey across the plains."

Brother Capson was a short man with a soft voice, obviously not Danish, but I understood his every word. His sincerity and kindness were evident as he spoke. "Perhaps you know my wife, Ingrid, and our two sons, Charles and John? We come from a small farming community near Malmo, Sweden, just across the Baltic Sea from Copenhagen.

"Sister Jasperson, have you met Sister Serena Evensen?"

"The name is not familiar, but if I saw her face I might recognize her."

"I will make sure you two sisters meet tomorrow. We have assigned Sister Evensen and her three children to be in the same wagon with your family. When Sister Evensen's personal items are loaded and the animals arrive you will be ready."

Serena and I had never talked before, but her face was very familiar. After we were introduced, I remembered. I remembered Serena's face, distraught with sorrow, from a particular morning prayer service on the *Benjamin Adams*. It was the day when Serena's four-year-old daughter had been buried at sea, just like I had buried my son, Mads.

Serena was from Norway, and most of the time the Norwegians stuck together. It was easier that way. From the moment I met her, all of my reservations about traveling together were gone. I knew we would become good friends. She was slightly taller than me, but a larger woman, with a strong determined jaw. Her personality was magic. Never mind our language differences, we each knew enough of Danish and Norwegian to communicate. Serena's oldest, Ingeborg, was nine. Her handsome six-year-old son was named Even, and her baby, Erastus, was two.

Serena was much busier than me, especially because of Erastus. How quickly I had forgotten the energy required to keep up with a two-year-old. As time allowed, Serena and I found time to get acquainted. "I married a fine man, Henrik Evensen. He was a sea captain, and we had five children together, three boys and two girls. In 1852 we were introduced to Mormon missionaries and we were baptized that same year. Henrick and I dreamed of going to Zion with our family, but my worst nightmare came true when Henrick drowned at sea during a great storm. Losing Henrick was a devastating loss for our family. Over time I adjusted to his loss, but I soon realized I would not find happiness unless I followed our dream to Zion.

"Leaving Norway was a difficult decision, Annie. My brother begged me, even tried to bribe me, not to go. I was not likely to ever see my mother again. I will never be able to visit the grave of my dear little son, who died when he was six. Torjus is buried next to the church in our little town of Risor. In my mind's eye, I can still see the day I left on the ship for Copenhagen. You remember it was winter when we left our homes for Copenhagen. The snow was six feet deep in Risor. I will never forget the silhouette of my dear mother, standing on the dock, wringing her hands and weeping as we pulled away."

I was struck by the similarities in our lives, and as far as I was concerned, there was no question why our families were chosen to travel together. *Yes, I am certain our two families will blend together just fine.*

"Moder! Moder!" Hans came running. "The herd of cows and oxen are coming! We can finally get started across the plains!" Hans was not the only one filled with excitement. I am certain that every single saint in our camp was eager to begin the last leg of our journey to Zion.

"Zion. Zion" The words tumbled over my tongue. I thought the worst was behind us, and that we would soon be welcomed by the saints into Zion. How naive of me.

Twenty-two

"Be very cautious around the oxen." John explained as the children gathered around, gazing at the animals. "I have precious little experience with oxen. I am told they are very methodical, yet strong enough to pull a loaded wagon. They appear to be gentle and docile, but I am not sure I believe that."

The children looked upon the beasts-of-burden with wondering eyes, intimidated by the size and apparent strength. "I have given them names." John explained. "These two are Duke and Thunder, the lead yoke. Back here are Buck and Baldy, the second yoke." Our confidence in John as the teamster would soon be tested, because, in a few days John would hitch the oxen to our wagon, and guide the team across the plains.

Duke and Thunder, Buck and Baldy, as well as the hundreds of other oxen purchased, were young castrated cattle. Most were about four years old and were shoed to protect their feet from the rocky terrain. The oxen were supposed to be trained with simple verbal commands. Commands such as "giddy-up, back, and whoa," as well as the more confusing commands of "gee (turn right) and haw (turn left)."

The oxen were paired using a wooden yoke especially designed to fit the neck and shoulder anatomy of cattle. We were told that oxen were much more efficient "pullers" than horses or mules. The science of "oxteamology" meant that the "bullwhacker" or teamster walked along on the left side of the lead oxen with a whip, prod or goad, shouting commands, and using body language to urge them on.

As a part of our "fittingout" we also had two "milch" cows. The children named them Klara and Lotte. We were all familiar with cows, having had one on the old farm. We even had a churn, so having fresh milk and butter again was heavenly. After milking the cows, I strained the milk to remove any debris. Then I solicited the help of the children. "Yern, could you please help me pour this cream into the churn? I believe it is your turn to make the butter today."

Churning was simple. The cream was agitated by a wooden dasher, causing the cream to turn frothy and finally into butter. After the new butter was made, it was necessary to separate the butter from the buttermilk so it would not spoil. We would wash the butter, add salt and store for future use. We saved the buttermilk and used it along with the "skimmed" milk for drinking or baking.

The campfire had burned down to orange embers by the time Serena and I finally relaxed from the day's busywork. "John says that we need to make haste in the morning. Brother Capson has planned a trial run for our division and we are to pack the wagon as if we were actually leaving. John will hitch up the oxen and cows to the wagon while we get everything packed."

"I will be ready." Serena smiled. "John does not need to worry about me being ready. I can barely sleep, I am so excited!"

"Our Division has a plan. A blast of a horn will wake everyone before daylight. We are to feed our families, clean and pack away supplies, hitch the cattle to the wagon and be ready to pull out as soon as possible."

Every family had their own plans, in order to be successful. John, Serena, Catherine and I talked about our plans in every detail. We each knew our own responsibilities. Although I was still not feeling totally healed from the effects of cholera, I agreed that I would milk the cows. Serena would wake the children. "I want to milk the cows, Moder. I know how. Please. Please" Hans begged.

I was reminded that Hans needed an important assignment, but I was not quite prepared to relinquish control of such an important task. "Hans, I have a better idea. Would you be willing to be in charge of the campfire? Every evening, you would gather enough wood for the next day, keep the wood covered and dry, in case it rains during the night, then start the fire early in the morning so we can prepare our meal. Once the fire is burning good, I would like you to help John yoke up the cattle."

"Yes, Moder, yes!" Hans's voice was filled with approval.

"Catherine, would you be in charge of Ingeborg? The two of you ladies could help Serena with the smaller children? By the time the children are up and dressed, I should be done with the milking. Then the four of us will prepare breakfast together. Once we have the food ready, we can call John and Hans, have morning prayers, and everyone can eat. Only after we have cleaned the pots and dishes can we start packing the wagons."

All the planning did not prepare us for the actual "doing." The first lesson we learned was that it took twice as long to get ready as we had anticipated. John's abilities were stretched to the limits when he tried to yoke the oxen together. He struggled to fix the wooden stick over each animal's necks, and then hitch them to the wagon tongue.

American ways seemed strange, I thought. I could not imagine how a wooden axle wagon, and oxen with a stick across their necks are going to get us across the Rocky Mountains. Most of the brethren had no greater skills than John, but with persistence and helping each other, the oxen were finally lined up and hitched to the wagon.

John had been milking our two cows prior to our leaving, but now I would take over. I was quite surprised how I had lost the special touch for milking. It took a certain amount of courage to balance on a three-legged-stool, and saddle up close to Lotte's udder. I talked to Lotte in a soft steady voice, stroking her side. I explained my intentions, and I warmed my hands before I felt her teats. "It is going to be okay, Lotte. Do not be afraid, old girl." I tried several different holds on the teat, finding the hold that was just perfect for Lotte. I began to squeeze and pull, releasing the steamy milk into my clean bucket. Lotte was a large gentle cow, with huge brown eyes. She waited patiently while I relieved her swollen glands. The process was so much slower than I had hoped, and I still had to milk Klara!

"Folks. I anticipated that we would have been ready to leave camp much earlier." Brother Capson spoke at the top of his voice. "I have double checked with everyone now, and it appears we are finally ready to depart. I will take the lead.

Each wagon should fall into the assigned order. We will head in a southwesterly direction, about one mile, before we make camp." From the angle of the sun, I could tell it was already the middle of the afternoon.

Brother Capson snapped his whip over the heads of his oxen, signaling the beginning. Ten teams of oxen and wagons pulled into a single line, forming one section of the soon-to-be larger wagon train. The teams of oxen were hot from the mid-day sun, but they pulled with all their might, straining against the weight of the wagons. The bullwhackers coaxed and prodded their charges with whips, shouting commands. The wagons maneuvered around tents, cattle, and a crowd of observers. "Giddy-up, Duke. Giddy-up Thunder! No, no! Not that way!" John shouted. "Haw, Duke! Haw!"

Our peaceful orderly camp turned into one of confusion and chaos. The brethren shouted commands to their own teams, unfamiliar Danish commands to the American trained oxen! There was a virtual orchestra of gees and haws, with whips snapping and popping overhead. Instead of the oxen pulling together as a team, they pulled every which direction, except for the one desired. Several oxen took off, leaving the bullwhackers behind. Several wagons toppled on their sides, spilling the contents, and women grabbed their children, screaming, and fleeing in every direction.

When the dust finally settled, a quick check of the camp revealed there were no injuries, but many of the wagons had broken tongues and axles. It was obvious we would be detained yet again, for needed repairs.

"What just happened?" Hans ask. He could not comprehend what he had seen.

Wanting to explain, but unable to speak, Serena began. "Hans, the oxen..." She tried to contain her response to the hilarious situation. It seemed as though laughing would be irreverent. However, Serena's full-blown belly laugh was not to be silenced. She saw the humor in the situation, and she started laughing; a double over, "slap-your-side" laugh, with "tears-running-down-your-cheeks" shrieking.

I am not sure that the children understood why Serena was laughing so hard, but they started laughing, too. I think they were actually laughing at Serena. Nevertheless, the laughing was contagious as poison oak. The laughter changed the atmosphere of our camp from gloom and tragedy, to one of lightened spirits. After all the detailed planning we had done, and the late night hours of discussing details, everyone had forgotten we emigrants spoke precious little English, and the oxen did not understand one single command in Danish!

Twenty-three

"Brothers and Sisters, the Peter Olsen Company will offi-cially begin moving tomorrow, after morning prayers." Our division gathered around Brother Capson, listening intent-ly. "We will be taking a new route to Fort Leavenworth, and breaking a new trail. The route promises to have plentiful grass, however, the route will also take us deeper into hos-tile territory. Do not worry! President Olsen has called five sturdy men to be armed guards."

A bugle echoed through the wagons at 4 a.m. on June 15, and the Scandinavian saints began their journey across Kansas, Wyoming, and into Utah territory. This was no tri-al performance. Each wagon was to be ready by 7 a.m. if circumstances allowed.

As teams readied, they pulled out, but our company was much later. Try as we might, with one delay after the other, it was nearly 4 p.m. before John signaled to our team that the time had come to pull. The oxen seemed a little more comfortable this day than the previous. John walked along-side Duke, a whip in his hand, and our family walked along-side the wagon. The cows, yoked together, and tethered to the wagon, brought up the rear.

As the wagon train formed into a single line, I glanced ahead, then back towards our old camp. All I could see, in either direction, were wagons snaking through the grass as tall as my waist. What an exhilarating sight. After weeks of waiting to be "fitted out," and with the sweltering afternoon sun on our backs, we were finally on our way.

"I am already tired, and we just got started." Serena sighed.

"We are all tired, but I feel quite energized, knowing we are on the move," I responded.

"Look out that direction. I can see for miles, and there is nothing but flat land covered with grass. At this pace, it is going to take a year to get to Fort Leavenworth."

"The oxen are so slow, Moder. Could Catherine and I walk ahead?"

"No! I want you to all stay together. Hopefully, come tomorrow, the wagon train will be a little more efficient."

The first day of our journey was a real test for the company. Travel was more difficult than any captain had anticipated. The prairie grass was beautiful, providing plenty of food for the cattle, but the grass presented unanticipated difficulties. The oxen had no trail or road to follow, making the pulling even more challenging. The wagons were so overloaded with the weight of supplies and luggage, that even a small child could barely find room to ride. Leaders had anticipated four oxen to be sufficient to pull any wagon, but after a single day, we had traveled just two miles!

"We are making camp here!" Brother Capson shouted as he rode past the wagons. "There is a clearing ahead with plenty of water. Start forming a circle."

The sweaty oxen strained and struggled to pull the farm wagons into a gigantic circle. They pulled into a tight formation, tight as possible, making a corral for the cattle and horses. The men unhitched the oxen, untethered the cows and led them to the watering hole. The women and children began the task of unpacking the wagons. Serena and I pulled and tugged, struggling to unload the tent and heavier equipment. *Get used to this, Annie.* I thought. *This will be your routine for days to come.*

Indeed, we did have a routine. The cattle were watered, the cows milked, and they were turned out to graze in the corral formed by the wagons. The children were given the responsibility of finding fuel enough to build a fire. After the meal was cooked, we ate, cleaned and prepared an area on the outside of the corral for erecting our tent. John would sleep on the ground under the wagon.

"No need to put out bedding for me. I am standing guard tonight." John finished his last bite of beans. "I will put up the tent for you."

Serena and I had never combined our families in a single tent until now. We snuggled together, two mothers and wall-to-wall children. I stared into the darkness. My mind drifted back to Denmark, to our little thatched-roof house; a time when our family was complete, and Jens was with us. It seemed so long ago, when Jens and I slept in the same bed with our six children, twisted around each other like pretzels. We felt safe, warm and loved. Now there was a new family, a blended family, sleeping together, like pretzels inside our shelter.

The second day on the prairie was slightly improved over the first. Pilots went ahead of the wagons with spades and shovels cutting down banks of creeks for easier crossing. Every family was a little faster with their preparations.

Yoking the oxen was somewhat easier for the men. Milking, cooking, cleaning and packing the wagon was a little easier for the women. However, we had major difficulties with the oxen. The wagons were heavy, even before the provisions were added. With the extra personal items, the load was almost impossible for two yokes of oxen to pull with any speed. We took a short break at noon, just long enough to rest the animals. We continued on through the heat of the afternoon, making camp for the night at Big Blue, traveling only eight miles total for the day.

"President Olson has called a meeting with all the brethren as soon as possible." Brother Capson shouted above the noise and commotion. "Please, men, gather in the field near the lead wagon."

The fire was still burning when John returned. I could not wait for him to begin. "What was that about?" I inquired.

"Annie, President Olsen says the speed of our wagon train must increase. If not, we could be caught in winter storms before we get into the Salt Lake Valley. With that in mind, President Olsen asks for donations to purchase additional oxen for each wagon. Several men have agreed to go back to Kansas City and locate the needed cattle. Meanwhile, we will remain camped here at Big Blue. President Olsen also ordered all saints to empty their wagons of any personal items unnecessary for the trek."

I was speechless. *Not my trunk. Not the finely detailed wooden trunk Jens had made and dragged halfway around the world. Never. I will never abandon my trunk!* The trunk held all our belongings; our clothing, the Bible, and the quilt mother had given to me. I never shared these feelings with Serena, nor did she approach me with hers. We chose to politely avoid the subject.

We waited through fierce frightening thunderstorms that turned our camp into sticky mud. The incessant winds blew around us, while we waited for the brethren to return. We were accustomed to waiting, but this time murmuring and impatience began slithering through the grass. Even though you could not see it, you knew it was there. "Brother Gustav told me he is going to leave the Company when we get to Fort Leavenworth." John stared into the fire pit. "Gustav says his children are still ill, and he is too tired to go on. He is going to stay behind in Missouri. I do not judge him or blame him. I might do the same thing. Annie, Serena. I hesitate to ask you ladies, but did you want me to help you unpack your trunks and remove them from the wagon?"

"I will be leaving my trunk in the wagon for now." Serena's voice was quick and defiant.

"I think we will be able to keep up with the rest of the wagons without removing our trunks," I responded. *I am certainly not removing my trunk if Serena is refusing to remove hers.* All I needed was an excuse to keep my trunk in the wagon.

Seven days later, on June 23rd, the men arrived with the additional oxen. Hitching up four oxen had been a challenge, but now John had six beasts to manage! "Hans." I began. "You have been a tremendous help for John, but with the additional oxen, he is going to depend on you more than ever."

"Yes, Moder. I will help John with the oxen. I will do whatever you ask." Hans was quick to respond.

Annie, I thought to myself, you have much to be thankful for. Did you notice how your son was quick to respond, in obedience and eager to assist? All you had to do was ask. How is it that you are so slow to be compliant?

We walked more than one week through giant foxtail and purple love-grass. We walked through grass still wet with dew, and grass hot from the blazing sun. Although we had the extra oxen, the traveling was made only somewhat easier. I was unable to judge the total distance we had traveled, but John thought we had only covered about ten miles a day.

One day seemed like the next, as we fell into a routine of rising early, praying, milking, cooking, packing the wagon, yoking up and "nooning." The afternoons were sweltering as we continued our walk, shaded only by the hats and bonnets we wore. We walked, tripping over ruts in the soil. We stumbled over our own skirts that became filthy from dragging in the grass. We walked until the evening when a camp was selected. Then evening chores began anew with gathering fuel, cooking, washing up, milking, mending, and socializing.

"Sisters, I am hesitant to speak to you about orders we received several days ago. I remind you that we were told to discard any items that might be putting unnecessary weight on our wagon." John's voice was firm as he looked directly at Serena and I. "I know how important your trunks are to you. I know you have pulled and pushed them all the way from your homeland. I must tell you, even though we now have Knut and Axel, the third yoke of oxen, our animals are struggling to keep up with the rest of the wagon train."

Serena and I surrendered, stuffing away our defiance, and with John's strength, we lifted our trunks from the wagon and on to the prairie grass. The very thought of leaving my precious trunk behind stirred up raw emotions. This was no ordinary trunk or simple wooden box. This trunk was the last tangible piece of home, the last item Jen's hands had crafted. I was emotionally unprepared to sever the strings of the past. I did not have a choice. John was telling us that unless we made the wagon's load lighter, our cattle would suffer and ultimately we might risk making the journey. I could not take the chance.

My fingers touched the trunk, worn with battle scars from our traveling. I loved the beautiful grain of the wood, and the memories tucked tightly inside. Carefully, rubbing my hand across the surface, I could almost feel Jen's fingers and the warmth of his flesh against mine. In my mind's eye, I could see Jens as he shaped the trunk that would take our family to Zion. How I longed to touch Jens's hands. I carefully folded our personal items, one by one, and tucked the clothing and treasures to the rear of the wagon. Serena silently folded her items and found a place to tuck them in the wagon box.

The air was still crisp, the dew yet hanging on the prairie grass, as our wagon train pulled out early the next morning. I glanced back for one last look. There in the grass, made flat by our camping, were two beautiful hand-carved trunks, amongst hundreds of treasures, lying strewn about the camp, abandoned by a multitude of compliant pioneers.

Twenty-four

Our people struggled through tall grass, over creeks and meadows, and through horrendous storms. On two different occasions, the wagon train traveled the wrong route, coming to a steep bluff, near the river. Murmuring and frustrations grew louder, because we were forced to spend another full day backtracking to correct our route. Backtracking was necessary in order to cross the deep, wide Kansas River at a specific point, usually frequented by the military.

The morning of July 9 began with the familiar sound of a bugle, signaling an early start of the river crossing. With picks and shovels, men began cutting away at a steep hillside, making a rough road for the wagons, cattle, and people to get down the hill to the river. The wagons were then lowered backward, with the wheels in a locked position. Heavy ropes and multiple hands held the weight of the wagons back until they reached the river's edge. Finally, the loaded wagons were ferried across the swift waters by means of additional ropes and pulleys.

Men on horseback herded the cattle through the swift current. Whips popped and snapped over the heads of the cows and oxen, as men shouted their commands to the frightened animals.

"Go ahead, Annie. We will be right behind you." Serena urged.

I grabbed hold of Yern's hand. "Catherine, hold on to Hans." We cautiously ventured over the rocky soil, slipping and sliding down the bank of the make-shift trail to the river's edge. Several times I nearly lost my balance, but was able to catch myself as we continued down the steep embankment.

"Climb inside. Our wagon is next." John helped us, one by one inside the wagon. "Try to distribute your weight around the wagon." We sat on top of supply boxes and between crates as the wagon floated and jerked along, until we reached the opposite side. My imagination ran rampant, fearing the absolute worst. Perhaps our wagon would be swept away by the swift current and we would flip over into the chilly waters. The possibility seemed quite real. It was not until we were safely deposited on the opposite bank that I could breathe without fear.

Although the distance across the river was not great, our company spent three arduous days crossing the Kansas River. This crossing was not without tragedy, however. The mighty jaws of the river claimed the life of a young man, about 18 years of age.

"John, I heard a young man died today. What happened?"

"He was helping to herd cattle across the river, and the horse he was riding stepped into a deep hole, throwing him off. I guess the guy could not swim very well, and he panicked. We tried to get to him, but the current was too fast. He was gone."

"Oh, John, I feel so sorry for his family. What a tragedy."

Our starting was made late once again because of a thunder and lightening storm that lasted most of the night. Once we started, walking was next to impossible as we slipped and slid through muck and mud, trying to keep our feet under us. The winds were relentless, blowing the bonnets of our heads, and threatening to destroy the bonnets of our wagons.

We had nearly froze during the night, but the oppressive heat during the day nearly caused us to pass out. Serena struggled to keep up the pace, because she carried her youngest child most of the way.

"Annie, I am exhausted. I think I shall not be able to carry Erastus one more step."

"Would you like John to stop so you can put Erastus inside the wagon?"

John understood. The oxen paused long enough for Serena to wrap her two-year-old Erastus in a blanket, and tuck her sleeping baby amongst the boxes and supplies in the front of the wagon. "Oh, that is so much better." Serena smiled. "Erastus will likely sleep two hours."

Serena and I walked slightly behind the wagon, holding hands of the smaller children, concentrating on our steps so we would not fall. We had traveled but a short distance when one of the front wheels of our top-heavy farm wagon slipped into a mud hole and toppled over. Serena and I watched in horror as the wagon flipped to its side. We were helpless to prevent the catastrophe and unable to reach little Erastus. Serena's screaming cries could be heard for miles. "My baby! My baby is in the wagon. Help! My baby!"

In a frantic pace to save Erastus, boxes, bags, and barrels were lifted from the wagon and with a mighty heave, the brethren pushed the wagon back on all four wheels. There lay the lifeless body of Serena's baby, face down in thick black mud. Snatching Erastus from the muddy hole, two brethren began the task of saving the little child.

Serena watched, wailing and screaming for God to save her child. I held Serena. Friends gathered around, but most were helpless. Two of the brethren worked on Erastus, cleaning the mud off his eyes, nose and mouth. For what seemed like forever, the brethren worked on Erastus, and Serena pled with God to save her child.

"He is breathing! Oh, God, he is breathing." At first Erastus took a slow shallow breath, then a full deep breath, and finally Serena's baby started crying. Erastus worked himself into such a protest of screaming and wailing assuring those around that God had indeed spared his life. I had never before witnessed such a miracle, for truly, it was a miracle that Erastus survived that day.

For the most part, the wagon train had continued on without us, and we had no time to delay, nor time to think about what had just happened. Clinging tightly to Erastus, Serena carried him until we camped for the night, and only then did we have the opportunity to properly thank God for His mercy.

It was July 22 when we struck the Old Emigration road by the Little Blue River, putting behind us 330 miles of treacherous trail on difficult terrain. We had taken 37 days to do so! What a price we paid for traveling without a trail in unchartered territory.

"We have located a good camp site just ahead. We will hold up for two days to make necessary repairs to wagons and observe the Sabbath." Brother Capson spread the news.

The next two days our company camped in a beautiful valley, close to the river, a paradise of nature covered with a wealth of wild flowers. Many of the flowers were familiar to me, but none were as beautiful as the plethora of rainbow-colored cactus blooms.

Saturday was filled with plenty of work for everyone. The men busied themselves repairing wagons and grazing the cattle. The women worked in camp, preparing food enough for Sunday. We mended and washed clothing. Most of all, we took advantage of the river to bathe the children, and then finally ourselves.

"Moder! Moder! Look what we found!" Hans held out his hands, overflowing with clumps of wild green grapes. "John and I found these in the grove of trees over there. Try them, they are so tasty."

"Oh, mother. These grapes are delicious. Please. Before we leave this camp, could Hans and I go pick more grapes?" Catherine plead.

"Yes, Catherine. I think that is a good idea, but we must be careful about eating too many. You might be sorry if you over-eat grapes while we are traveling."

Sunday was a day for resting and praying. We sang familiar songs of praise and savored the words from our spiritual leaders. We rejoiced in the river baptism of a young woman, and we lifted our voices to the heavens, singing with angelic harmony. I had not heard Serena sing until then. Never before, nor have I heard since, such a voice of pure sweetness. Serena's voice was magical. Her voice carried over the others, echoing out into the flowering hills. She sang from her heart to the God that had brought us this far, and most especially to the God that had saved the life of little Erastus.

"Serena, your voice is beautiful. I could listen to you sing all day."

"Thank you, Annie. You are so kind."

"I am trying to tell you, Serena, that I would give almost anything to have a voice like yours."

The evening was filled with a spirit of celebration and relief throughout our camp. We lingered with friends to fellowship. "Margarethe, it is so good to see you again. How are you?"

"Annie, Brother Lars and I are getting along quite well, thank you. We have had our trials, as you well know, but it is good to remember that in the greatest season of suffering, we have the greatest cause to rejoice. It is when we endure what we thought impossible, we find those were our happiest moments. Remember, Annie, we were not promised this journey would be easy." Margarethe's arms held me in an embrace. "It is wonderful to talk with you, and learn your family has healed. Be well, my friend."

"Annie, how good it is to see you again." Brother Mads Powelson reached out his hand, looking directly into my eyes. "You are looking very well."

Mads and I had seen each other in passing, but we had not spoken; not since our company of Danes had been deposited on the pier at Westport. We had not spoken since the night Jens and I shared our meal with Mads's family, in St. Louis. I recalled how he and his family stood grieving over the loss of Dorothea, Mad's wife, and the children's mother. Mads and I had not spoken since cholera claimed the life of my dear husband, and nearly claimed the life of my children and myself.

Mads and I had so much we could have talked about, but we did not. It was the way Mads took my hand as he looked deep into my eyes, smiling and continuing to hold my hand longer, that touched my heart. "I am doing well, Mads. Quite well, thank you. How are you and your family?"

Twenty-five

Walking seemed easy once we reached the emigrant trail on the 22nd of July. The trail was well worn from the hundreds of wagons and thousands of tired feet, having traveled this same route on the north side of the Platt River. The trail wandered close to the river at times, and away from the river through deep canyons at others, exposing us to dangerous areas. The trail passed through a beautiful landscape of rivers and trickling streams, crisscrossing the land, and nowhere was a single house or cultivated land to be seen. We saw an abundance of deer and wildlife, including huge rattlesnakes that frightened us all, but the real threat came from the wild-people occupying this land, the Indians.

"Listen up people! We are in Indian Territory. We have doubled our armed guards, and everyone must be cautious at all times. Stay with the company and do not wander off." Brother Capson spread the warning. "If we have any trouble, be prepared to hide the young children inside the wagons."

The next day we came in sight of a camp with thousands of Sioux Indians. Our leaders, recognizing we must pass right through them, were also impressed that the natives were our friends. The Indians gathered in their own horses and made room for our wagons and cattle to feed. We passed through them, much to our surprise, without incident. We made our camp a short distance beyond. It seemed as though the Indians paid us no attention.

"Do not be fooled," John warned. "Indians have been prowling around our camp, so we are going to double the guards while we camp here."

I lay inside our tent, my body aching from the long hot day, and my thoughts filled with apprehension. Warnings crowded in my head, warnings given weeks before. Warnings of savage native red-men, and their random vicious attacks on innocent white people. The killings were unprovoked; killings of innocent emigrants, that had become separated from the larger group. Oh, how I wished I could discuss my concerns with Serena, but I felt best to keep silent. No need to give voice to my fears. *Oh, Lord. Protect and keep us from harm.*

It was mid-day, about a day past Fort Kearney, one of many insignificant military posts along the trail, that our company was ordered to halt.

"Listen, everyone! Listen up!" Brother Capson screamed. "We need to pull our wagons into a tight circle and corral the cattle immediately."

Without any warning, Catherine began panicking, screaming, and shouting "The Indians are coming. The Indians are coming." Her screaming startling everyone including Serena.

"Hurry, John. Get the animals unhitched and inside the corral. The Indians must be coming." Serena shouted.

The panic was so contagious that I, too, felt the fear. When I tried to speak, my voice began quivering. "Ch-children. S-s-stay close to our wagon. Do not wander away."

John and Hans responded with haste, not once questioning Brother Capson's orders. We had barely pushed our company wagons together, and secured the cattle inside when we beheld a most spectacular site. Off in the distance, covering the prairie like waves of the sea, tens of thousands of buffalo moved in unison directly toward our camp. The massive beasts of the prairie moved closer and closer; and the roaring of their feet pounding on the desert floor was deafening. Had we continued, our wagons would have been destroyed, because the buffalo never stopped or diverted from their intended route.

Several of our brethren did shoot after them. The dust was so thick that we could not see wagons, men or buffalo, for about fifteen minutes. When the dust settled, 22 fine buffalo had been killed by our men, killed near our camp, as if God himself had brought them to us by a miracle!

Every adult busied themselves caring for the meat and smiling at our good fortune. The men skinned and butchered, and the women prepared the meat to dry. I looked closely at one of the massive brown beasts, with the magnificent head and large innocent eyes. The thought came to me, *kings and wealthy men would have gladly paid a great fortune to see what we had just seen.*

" I was so certain the Indians were coming to attack us. I am sorry if I frightened you all." Catherine apologized.

John reminded us. "This experience should remind us that we must always follow orders without question. Brother Capson did not have time to explain every detail and wait for any questions. It is for our own safety that we must obey without question."

"I agree. Our wagon train would have been destroyed, had we not pulled back and made camp." Hans's eyes were fixed on the skeleton of a monstrous buffalo. "Look at the size of this giant."

Our company moved on without incident, finding creeks and streams to make a camp, and holding over on the Lord's Day for meetings and worship. The Sabbath was a day for physical resting as well as spiritual rejuvenation. However, this particular Sabbath day was a celebration. We received a wagon full of Mormon leaders traveling east from Zion towards St Louis. Taking advantage of our guest's knowledge and words of wisdom, we held camp an additional two days. Among the church leaders was a beloved familiar figure, Brother Erastus Snow, the President of the Scandinavian Mission when we were converted.

Understanding precious few words of English, we politely listened to the preaching, but we were most excited to hear from President Snow. Speaking in our native tongue, he lifted our broken hearts and spirits, encouraging us to endure to the end "Do not be disheartened nor lose sight of your goal. You are so very close to reaching Zion. I promise you, when you see the great valley of Salt Lake, you will not be disappointed. God has chosen each of you, individually and collectively for this day of building Zion. You sweet, precious Scandinavians are the very people needed to build communities in the valley of promise, high in the Rocky Mountains."

We were filled with renewed hope and thankfulness to our God. In the evening we witnessed a young man and woman united in marriage, and we older folks socialized, while the young people danced. Oh, how I loved the music of the fiddle, the merrymaking and singing with joyful celebration. If, but for a brief moment, I felt the joy and spark of my youth.

"Good evening, Sister Jasperson." Mads Powelson bowed his head, greeting me kindly. "Sister Evensen, how are you this fine day?" Mads's conversation was simple, inquiring of our health and our families.

"I am not sure if you heard, Brother Powelson, but we had an accident with our wagon. Little Erastus was pinned beneath in the mud." Serena explained. "Thanks to God he was revived and seems to have recovered quite well. How are you managing with your family?"

Mads did not linger long, keeping his conversation polite, but I could not help wondering if Mads had a motive other than just being social. Feelings of awkwardness surfaced again, but perhaps I had it all wrong. Perhaps it was Serena, the beautiful blonde Norwegian, attracting Mads to our camp again?

We became fascinated by unusual rock formations like Courthouse Rock and Jail-house Rock. It was Chimney Rock, the most well known landmark to the West that marked the end of the prairie and the beginning of more rugged and steep terrain. We watched the single-spired natural monument for three days before we camped alongside the 400-foot column, known as Chimney Rock. The rock column looked like a haystack with a tall pole sticking far above its top. "We will be having extra guards tonight for the cattle," John explained. "The cattle seem to be skittish." Even though our company had posted extra guards, our cattle still managed to scatter during the night, forcing us to stay in camp an extra day, while the men found the wayward animals.

While in camp we prayed together and received further instructions around flickering campfires. Brother Capson gave additional directions. "We will soon be passing Fort Laramie. This fort is on the south side of the Platte River at the foot of the Black Hills and marks the point 550 miles west of the Missouri River. Two years ago the government of the States entered into a treaty with the Sioux Indians occupying these lands. The purpose of the Fort Laramie Treaty was to assure safe passage for the whites along the Oregon Trail. As a part of the treaty, the United States Military built this fort. It is occupied by approximately 200 soldiers.

"People, listen to me! It is critical that we keep the wagons as close together as possible. It is also essential that every oxen and cow be kept together. Do not allow your cattle to stray, as we will be passing through land occupied by approximately 4,000 Brule and Oglala Sioux Indians."

We moved on, having traveled but two or three days, when the same church leaders that had been with us returned. "They are requesting we send help to a struggling English company behind us," John said. "Brother Capson inquired of our brethren if there are volunteers to take 15 yokes of oxen back to the English. It seems many of their oxen have been lost."

"Did you volunteer to go, John?" I tried to keep my voice calm but was certain that John sensed my fear of the very thought of driving our oxen and managing without him.

"I did indicate my willingness to help, but Brother Jensen and Brother Bentsen were chosen."

"That is good." I was relieved. *I need you here, John. Oh, how we need you with us.*

It was mid-August, perhaps the 17th when we passed a large encampment of Indians, just before we reached Fort Laramie. We were camped, our wagons in tight formation as instructed, but a couple of our cows wandered away. No one knew for certain, as the stories had many versions, how two cows belonging to our company were shot and killed by an Indian named High Forehead.

This shooting caused great concern among our people, who were fearful of further acts of aggression by the Indians. Armed guards were doubled as we camped at noon, and the incident was reported to Lieutenant Grattan, at the Fort. The owners of the cows insisted that the Indians provide some sort of retribution for the deed. Chief Conquering Bear came forward and offered a horse as payment, but Lieutenant Grattan refused the offer. Without any resolution for the senseless killing of two cows, our company moved on.

We pushed onward, with every man, woman, and child on high alert. Extra guards were posted, and four days passed before Brothers Jensen and Bentsen caught up with our company again. Their safe arrival brought much relief for their families, especially when the brethren gave vivid details of what had happened at Fort Laramie.

Brother Jensen explained. "The Brule camp had been merrymaking when the cows were shot and the Indians ate the meat. Lieutenant Grattan would not back down on the arrest of High Forehead, and he rode into the Brules' camp with 28 troops and two 12-pound howitzers, looking for trouble. Chief Conquering Bear, the spokesman for all the Sioux, tried to defuse the situation, but Grattan and his men were looking for a fight. When Chief Conquering Bear turned to walk away, a young inexperienced soldier shot and killed the Chief. Both sides opened fire. The military cannons were aimed too high, causing little damage to the Indian camp, but within minutes, all the white soldiers were killed except for one. The one surviving soldier had his tongue cut out and he later died at the fort."

Based on recommendations from Brother Jensen and Brother Bentsen, who expected a full-blown war with the Indians, our company crossed the river and joined the Richardson Company. The Richardson Company had also started their journey from Westport, leaving a few days prior to our departure. Their company consisted of about 40 wagons and 270 people.

Every company of emigrants became concerned over the Sioux Indian fight with the soldiers from Fort Laramie. All with whom we came in contact, spoke of the Indian incident. Although the details varied, it was clear that traders were fleeing, expecting a war. During the night, several smaller parties came into our camp, begging to be allowed to stay with us. "For God's sake, Mr. Richardson, give us shelter, for the Indians are after us." From that date, and for several days after, we traveled with the Richardson Company, making larger, and therefore, safer camps at night.

"Serena, I am so frightened. I walk in fear all the day long that our camp will be attacked, and I can not sleep at night." I finally voiced my concerns. "How are you doing?"

"Annie, we all share the same fears. However, we are mighty in number, which should discourage the savages. Be careful not to let fear occupy too much of your day."

"Moder. Do not worry. John will take care of us. He has become quite a marksman, in case he has not told you."

With every step we took, we watched for signs of movement across the land. *What was that on the horizon? Did I see something move over there? What was that noise? Was that cry from a bird or an Indian?* All day long we wished for the evening, when we would make our camp for the night. We felt somewhat safer when we circled together and kept within the confines of the group. We ate our supper and prayed together, but I continued my prayers all night. Sleep? *Oh, sleep, where are you hiding?* Where could I find the deep, and restful sleep that would allow my aching body to heal? The much-needed sleep was crowded out because visions of 30 young soldiers lying dead on the ground, their bodies desecrated, and their heads scalped, danced in my head.

Twenty-six

The South Platt River was buffalo territory. Some days we did not see a single buffalo, but the next day we would see a hundred thousand of these wild cattle, filling an area over two miles long and a mile wide. At times our men shot at them to clear the trail for the wagons, but the shooting was not to kill the beasts. We were not in need of the meat at the time. We were, however, in dire need of fuel for fires, and the buffalo provided exactly what we needed; excrement or dung.

"Sisters, the buffalo have given us a most desirous source of fuel. Gather up the dried piles of 'buffalo patties' and build your fire. You might find that you enjoy the taste of a piece of meat cooked on these chips. Your food will not require pepper!" Brother Capson chuckled as he gave us directions.

A great number of sisters were repulsed with the thought of cooking with buffalo dung. "I will not be picking up dried dung and using it for cooking our food. I would rather eat raw meat than to use buffalo chips for my fire." Serena was emphatic. Although I was hesitant at first, particularly of the smell permeating our food, I soon realized the goodness and took advantage of the benefits.

"Hans and Yern, make sure you pick up the patties that are completely dry in the center. Wet chips do not burn very well."

During the night we were overtaken by yet another violent thunderstorm. The noise and clapping rolled across the prairie like a freight train. The sultry black night was filled with massive bolts of lightning, turning the darkness of our tents into a momentary brightness like the mid-day sun. Rain poured down, running inside our tent, soaking our bedding and forcing us to flee from the intended shelter. Wolves, coyotes, and buffaloes howled and bellowed all around us, silenced only by the sounds of gunfire from our men shooting at them.

I screamed at the children, trying to make my voice heard above the clamor of the night. "Climb inside the wagon! Hustle up! Find a place to sit on a box or a barrel, but just get inside."

"We can not all get in here. There is no room to sit down." Yern complained.

"If you can not sit, you can surely find a place to stand."

Eventually, daylight came, and the storm moved on, dumping its violence on some other poor company of emigrants, traveling the trail behind us. The silence of the prairie returned once again, and we were forced to lay over another day. We dried our clothing, put our belongings back together, and looked for the items that had disappeared during the night.

We had only gone about six miles when the trail crossed the Platt River. Brother Capson rode alongside our wagon, shouting out orders. "We will be making camp just ahead. Our company will start crossing the river early in the morning. Every family must stay together, crossing the river when your wagon crosses."

We felt a little more confident since we had crossed the Kansas River, but this time we would not be ferried across, we would be walking across. Brother Capson continued. "The river is about a half mile wide, and unless you are too ill or elderly to walk, you will need to wade through the waters."

The river crossing was exhausting and dangerous. The brethren struggled to get all the wagons across the Platte. At times it took 24 oxen, chained and roped together, just to pull one wagon across. The brethren worked together for two long tedious days, moving our company through the river to the opposite bank.

Fathers held their smaller children in their arms and waded through the chilly water, back and forth, over and over. In most cases, the women waded through, on their own. "Catherine, please hold hands with Hans. Yern, I want you between Catherine and me." Linking our hands together, with my youngest next to me, we crossed the river. We waded deeper and deeper through the current, until the water was up to Yern's chin. I tried to make conversation as if words would keep the children from being frightened. "Yern, you are doing great. We only have a short distance to go."

"The water is getting too deep, Moder. My feet are not touching the bottom. I feel like I am floating!"

"Just hang on to our hands, Yern. Do not let go."

"You need not worry, Moder. I have hold of Yern." Catherine assured me.

I silently prayed as we stepped through the slippery rocks, struggling to keep our footing. *Help us, oh Lord, to cross this river safely.*

From behind me, I began hearing the angelic voice of Serena, singing a sweet, familiar hymn.

> *"Come thou font of every blessing,*
> *Tune my heart to sing thy grace,*
> *Streams of mercy, never ceasing,*
> *Call for songs of loudest praise.*
> *Teach me some melodious sonnet,*
> *Sung by flaming tongues above.*
> *Praise the mount, I'm fixed upon it.*
> *Mount of God's unchanging love."*

Serena held hands with little Ingeborg, singing and maneuvering through the current, while two of the brethren carried Even and Erastus alongside Serena to the opposite shore.

Once again, Serena had used her voice to bring calm to a frightening situation. I was reminded once more of a scripture that had been read in our morning prayer meeting. "... be filled with the Spirit, speaking to one another in psalms and hymns and spiritual songs, singing and making melody in your heart to the Lord, giving thanks always for all things to God the Father in the name of our Lord Jesus Christ..."(Ephesians 5:18-20)

Our company camped on both sides of the Platt that night, finishing the crossing late in the afternoon of the second day. The last wagon had barely crossed the river when nine Indians came riding into our camp. They were unarmed and dressed alike, that is to say, they were nearly naked.

They had long black hair and the only coverings on their bodies was a piece of animal hide and a cloth across their shoulders, reaching below their knees. Another piece of hide was tied across their abdomen.

Even though the Indians held no weapons, everyone in camp became considerably frightened. Perhaps the savages were here to spy on us, only to return with weapons later. "Ingborg! Hurry! Hide in the wagon." Serena snatched up Erastus and stuffed her children out of sight. Catherine and the boys rushed to my side, frightened at the sight of such wildness. John frantically rushed for his rifle.

We watched while President Olson and another brethren, who knew some of the language of this tribe, stepped forward to meet the Indian chief. Through the interpreter, it seemed we had nothing to fear. The Indians were on their way to fight against another tribe, however, the Chief's demands of us were made clear. He wanted food and gifts for crossing their land. "Please, brethren. Put down your weapons" President Olson shouted. "They wish us no harm."

No harm? Did they mean us no harm? How could we feel at ease by a few simple words from a handful of Indians, when off in the distance, we could see hundreds of Indians, waiting on their horses. Within minutes an additional group of 19 Indians rode into our camp, joining their Chief. Dust swirled around the feet of the naked men. They dismounted their horses and began walking among us, pointing, jabbering and grunting to each other.

I held my breath as two large Indians walked directly towards our wagon.

Catherine held on to me from behind, hiding her body behind my skirts and hoping to also hide her eyes. Yern's curiosity far outweighed his fear as he held onto my skirt, examining every part of the red-man's nakedness. Instead of Hans clinging to me, he stood tall and mustering all his courage, he stepped forward with John and the two men demonstrated their intentions to protect our family.

Closer and closer the Indians came, jesting and pointing at Serena and me. My body turned cold. Even the goose-bumps on my arms trembled in terror. Then my thoughts returned to the lesson I had learned from Serena, just hours before. *Start singing. Sing, Annie. Sing.*

Soft at first, my voice shaky and off-key, I began singing from the depth of my soul. I called on the heavens in song. "Think not when you gather in Zion" I began, "Your troubles and trials are through." Serena's beautiful voice joined mine, then Catherine's voice joined ours and we all sang together. "That nothing but comfort and pleasure are waiting in Zion for you."

We sang through our fear and angst, gaining courage and strength with each phrase. Like ripples on water, voices of Scandinavia joined together, building a chorus across the camp, singing the verses one by one. "No, no 'tis designed as a furnace, all substance, all textures to try, To burn all the wood, hay and stubble, the gold from the dross purify."

Not a single Saint was harmed by the Indians that day, but no one trusted the natives, especially President Olson.

Fearing for our lives, we gave of our depleted supplies to pay the Chief and his people, praying that our generosity would keep peace with this tribe. In total, the Indians hauled away nearly 100 pounds of coffee, over 50 pounds of sugar and pork, two sacks of flour, some pocket knives, mirrors and a small barrel of gunpowder. With this, the Indians were satisfied, and they rode off.

Every man of our company stood guard that night, armed and waiting for the Indians to return. We believed the savages would take advantage of our vulnerability, striking us under the cover of night. Serena and I arranged our family inside the tent, placing our trust in the brethren to protect us. I lay awake with thoughts of the day crowding my mind, listening for unusual sounds or activity. The silence was deafening, broken only by cries from a pack of coyotes. I waited and I prayed. I knew fear could rule the night, stealing my peace and rest. So as before, yet in my mind, I began singing hymns and songs I had learned from years before.

Daylight was barely alive when the familiar sound of the bugle rang out, calling our camp alive. Sounds from the horn brought welcome assurance that we were yet alive. "Good morning children! Wake up. It is time for morning prayers and breakfast."

John was yoking the oxen and Serena and I were packing the wagon when the Indians returned. My legs felt like they would crumble and my heart started racing. I could clearly see a group of approximately 400 hundred armed Indians, led by the Chief, riding towards our camp. As they came to the river's edge, the larger group stopped, and about 50 or so continued through the river, riding into our camp. The red-men shouted and hollered, raising their weapons and making noises enough to scare any person. The Indians, as well as their wild horses, were decorated with different colors of fabric and hides, tied about their bodies.

"Relax people. Calm yourselves." Brother Capson shouted as loudly as he could. "No need to arm yourselves brethren, these Indians mean us no harm. The Chief has come in friendship."

Friendship was signified by a fabric headband. The headband was beaded with pearls and a green twig. He wore a dark red jacket, beaded with pearls, and his shoes were of deerskin. The finely adorned Chief dismounted his wild pony and addressed our leaders. They had come to thank us for the gifts and to show us they were friendly.

Not a single individual was entirely convinced the Indians meant us no harm. We all knew the Indians did as they pleased. They roamed where ever they liked, stealing from emigrants while pretending to be friends. I was convinced our leaders were inspired to offer the Indians more food as the enticement for our safe keeping. Serena and I gave the remaining bread from our morning meal, the bread intended for our lunch. Through the collective efforts, President Olsen found enough pork and bread to give every Indian a piece of each. Pleased and satisfied, the Indians left our camp, crossing the river to join their comrades on the opposite bank.

Twenty-seven

*T*he crossing of the Platte River marked the end of the prairie and the gateway to the desert, a land of rugged hills, and desolate terrain. The distance from Fort Laramie to the Sweetwater River was days and days away, perhaps nine or ten. The winds burned our faces, and the lack of adequate drinking water was broken only by more landmarks of rock formations and wide valleys. As far as we could see, the land was filled with sagebrush, and with rugged snow-capped mountains nearly surrounding us.

We trudged through the Iron Creek area and camped near Oil Mountain. We walked through Poison Springs Creek and strained to keep up with the wagon train over the ridge past the Avenue of Rocks. We walked and walked, dragging our bodies and wagons through Willow Springs, across Prospect Hill, camping again near Fish Creek and Greasewood Creek.

Day after day we went through the same process; morning meals, loading the wagon, and walking through sandy soil and tumbleweeds. We broke briefly at noon. We walked again for hours straining to put one foot ahead of the other. Our lips were chapped and swollen, our feet bleeding from blisters. We walked until a camp area was located, only to repeat the process the next day, and the next. Everyone suffered from the monotony and deprivations of this stretch of God-forsaken land, including the cattle.

Strewn along the trail were the remains of cattle and oxen, unable to survive the brutal desert. Bleached white bones, some covered with meat and hide, not finished off by the wolves or coyotes, were obvious reminders how vulnerable and weakened the animals had become. "Do you think our oxen will make it to the Sweetwater, John?" I inquired.

"I can not say, Sister Jasperson. However, I can tell you that Duke is suffering. I am concerned about the oxen, but I am more concerned about you and the children."

It was impossible to avoid the thoughts that crowded in my brain, poking and prodding at my will to survive. With every aching step, I wondered if my family would have enough food and water to reach Zion? I imagined having just a small piece of buffalo meat to chew. Sadly, I remembered how we had tried to dry the meat when it was provided, and how most of it had spoiled.

We passed the graves of emigrants, marked with mounds of dirt and covered with rocks or brush. Names and dates were scratched on rough markers. There were names of babies who had only a small chance of survival. There were adult names, unable to survive illness, or simply unable to survive the arduous physical demands of the trek.

Thoughts of survival were greatest when we arose each morning. Serena and I were forced to feed our families with precious little supplies. Every frigid morning I was reminded there would be but little milk if any. Without grass and water, our two milk cows were unable to provide.

I watched Catherine as her fingers mixed the flour with the fat, careful not to spill the precious powder for our morning biscuits. "Serena. What are we to do? You know, we ate the pork and dried fruits many weeks ago. We could possibly stretch the beans out another week, but the barrel of flour has but a few cups remaining in the bottom."

"We must first feed our children," Serena responded quietly. "We can go without."

Serena and I agreed we would combine our efforts, beginning with our morning prayer. Serena began, "Oh Heavenly Father, Lord of all, please hear our prayers. We are thankful for each and every day. We are thankful to be a part of this company, and for the inspired leaders, that guide us. We are thankful to be mothers of these six beautiful children. Lord, You must know that we have precious little food to feed our family. We ask for Thy tender mercy. Provide for us sufficient food, so that we may all live to see Zion, and not perish in the attempt."

I ended the prayer, pleading with God for the necessary food and water to feed our family. Serena and I then began fasting together, mentioning not a word to others. We pretended to eat our morning meal but saved the food for another time. Throughout the day we kept a prayer on our lips, and nothing but water in our stomach. To some, it might have seemed strange, to intentionally fast at a time like this. However, scriptures teach us to fast. Fasting is a means to master our appetites, to elevate the spirit within us, and build our spiritual faith in God.

I thought I had known hunger before, but I had never known hunger like this. At times I felt delirious, my head spinning and pounding with a fierce headache. I tripped and stumbled over my own legs, but nevertheless, Serena and I continued to fast. We prayed all day for God to hear our prayers and provide the "manna" necessary for our survival.

The wagon trail went through a large dry lakebed, covered with a white alkaline crust called "saleraetus." At first glance, I thought God had literally provided "manna" in the desert, as He had done for Moses and his people. Brother Capson spread the word. "Gather what you can of the white powder and use it as a substitute for baking powder." We gathered the white powder, but this was not the needed food we had prayed for.

Wondrous natural rock formations measured our progress along the trail and Independence Rock was one of the most anticipated unusual landmarks we would see. The granite rock, shaped like a beached whale, was not only known for its unusual rock appearance but was also known as the place where the trail met the Sweetwater River. Once rested, we would study the rock's estimated 5,000 names carved in the haystack formation. As high as one could see, completely around the massive rock, were thousands of pioneer's names. They were etched into history, pioneer "calling cards," left for the thousands more who would follow.

Next to Independence Rock, was the long-awaited, well known, Sweetwater River. As the lead wagons first caught a glimpse of the Sweetwater, shouts of relief could be heard for miles. "Hallelujah" and "Praise the Lord" echoed across the desert again and again. We had found cool, clear water for drinking, and green, grassy areas for the cattle! We drank freely of the sweetness, soaking up the refreshing relief.

The cattle were released to drink and cool themselves, then they were herded to an area to feed.

Serena and I were unloading the wagon when we heard a familiar voice. It was our kind friend, Brother Capson. "Can I help you sisters?"

"Yes. Oh, thank you, Brother Capson. Yes." I replied. "We would welcome the use a strong arm with this dirty heavy tent."

Brother Capson pulled the tent from our wagon and deposited it on the ground. All the while he smiled and chatted about the campsite. " We are so fortunate to find clear, clean water. Sisters, you will want to pick a site for your tent that is level and free from rocks, if possible. We will be camping here several days while our company mends broken wagons, and allows our cattle to recover. We need to reorganize our efforts, and for that reason, I come to you today.

"It has come to our attention that food supplies have become critically low for many families. President Olson has asked me to contact every family under my supervision, for the purpose of taking an inventory of food and supplies. "Would you allow me to take an inventory of your food?"

Serena was quick to reply. "You will not find much, Brother Capson. We have hardly a cup of flour left."

Brother Capson shook his head, silently conveying his empathy, as he jotted some notes on a piece of paper. "Thanks, sisters. I will report to President Olson." Moving on, Brother Capson walked to the next wagon, gathering the grim news that many families were in the same precarious position as we were.

President Olson presided over our company-wide prayer meeting the next morning. Everyone capable of walking gathered near President Olson's wagon, anxious to partake of the emblems of the sacrament. Many of our sick received blessings for recovery, and a newborn was given a name and a blessing of strength and health.

We were lifted in spirit with words of hope. "Brothers and Sisters," President Olsen continued. "Welcome to this gloriously beautiful day. It has come to my attention that many families are suffering for want of food. After making a complete inventory last evening, we have asked those families with extra food to bring their donations to my wagon. We will be redistributing the food to those in need this morning. No family should be suffering for want of food. I have also sent two of our brethren ahead on horseback, to inform Brigham Young of our critical situation."

"Eat, Annie and Sophia. Feed your children." Brother Capson continued, "This should be enough food to feed your family for now."

God answered our prayers with food gifts: a small piece of dried meat, additional flour, and beans enough for several meals. With the food and water, our weary bodies began healing.

We held over in the Sweetwater camp for five days. Our wise leaders knew the next part of the trail would demand more physical challenges than we had ever known, so resting was critical in the preparation. On the third evening, the annoying winds ceased their nagging presence, and our people gathered for what our leaders called a "traditional Independence Day celebration." We clapped along to the rhythm of favorite fiddle tunes while the youth danced. We filled the evening air with merrymaking and renewed friendships that had been too long ignored.

"Karen, oh my sweet friend. It is wonderful to see you." I looked into Karen's deep-set eyes, looking for a glimmer of joy. We had not talked privately since Karen's only child had died in the Westport camp. "Tell me, how are you and your husband?"

"Thank you for asking, Annie. Jens and I are so thankful to be a part of this emigration company. However, I still wake in the mornings, sometimes thinking I hear Martha crying. I miss her little smile, Annie. How I ache to hold her again. I find solace in the promise that I will hold her again in the life hereafter. Right now, we are thrilled just to have our faces looking towards Zion.

"Remember, Jens suffers from some physical limitations, and at times he can barely put one foot ahead of the other. I never hear him complain. He is such a spiritual man, and his weakness has made him strong. Jens is an example to everyone he meets of faith in God. But enough about me. Tell me how you are managing without your husband?"

Our women mingled around the campfires in their freshly washed, homespun dresses. The camp buzzed with conversations; questions and responses filled with emotional honesty. I loved being a part of the sisterhood of these women. We did not socialize frequently, usually staying in our family groups, but we could be apart for lengths of time, and when we came together, we were like family. We spoke as if there had not been a moment that separated us from the last gathering.

"Sister Jasperson." Mads extended his hand towards mine. "How good to see you again."

I did not recognize Mads at first glance. A dark hat shadowed his face, and he hid behind a full beard, hiding any familiar facial features. "Oh, Mads, it's you!" I managed a smile and grasp his hand. "I am sorry. I did not recognize you at first. How is your family?"

"Oh, Annie, could I talk with you? I need your advice."

Mads began a pitiful explanation of his struggles without Dorthea. "What am I to do, Annie? Every day I am responsible to keep the oxen fed and watered in a desert of sagebrush, barren of water. Every day I am required to keep the wagon in good repair, without the necessary tools and equipment to do so. I am required to keep my children safe and fed with food supplies that have dwindled down to nothing." Mads hesitated, unable able to speak, his eyes filling with emotion. "I do not believe I can continue another day, Annie."

Nothing could bring tears to my eyes quicker than an emotional man. Mads was pathetic and broken, completely lost without his wife, lover, and caregiver of his family. I responded as only I knew how.

"It is okay, Mads." I put my arms around him. "I understand, Mads. You know, I understand what you are going through." There in the dark of the desert, under the glistening stars, we comforted each other in a long, warm embrace.

CHAPTER 28

$\mathcal{U}$nusual rock formations became well known land-marks along the trail. Each landmark seemed more magnificent than the last, and Devil's Gate was no exception. The unimaginable solid rock formation had canyons, rising hundreds of feet high, carved by the Sweetwater River. The river rolled, tumbled and roared through the canyon like thunder, for about one and a half miles. Thankfully, the wagon trail, unlike the river, diverted around and not through the center of the monstrous rock.

As important as the Sweetwater was to our survival, the river presented a challenge of significant magnitude. The river, instead of running a more direct path, snaked back and forth in immense wide loops. The trail was clearly marked on one side of the river, but no wagon train could take the chance of following all of the river's loops, and staying on the trail. If we had, it would have taken us many more days than it did. Therefore, we were forced to travel in a more direct route, crossing the river over and over again until we reached the South Pass, which was the last camp on the Sweetwater. We crossed the freezing waters at least once a day.

Four days of travel took us into Split Rock territory, another natural landmark. It was in this territory, trying to avoid five different crossings that our company struggled through miles and miles of deep sandy soil. Our oxen, exhausted beyond comprehension, strained to pull the heavy wagons, but were held back by the soft earth.

"There is nothing we can do to help lighten the load of the wagon. We have already thrown out most everything that adds weight. I did not throw out the extra feather tick, but I do not think that would make any difference."

"Yes, Annie. I am thankful we decided to toss out heavy items, like our trunks. Even then, without the extra yoke of oxen, we would have never been able to keep up."

It was on September 12, while at Three Crossings, the third crossing of the Sweetwater, that relief came in the form of a single wagon, loaded with supplies from Great Salt Lake City. One single wagon of food could not begin to feed us, but as promised, the messengers sent to the Utah Valley had returned with a load of freshly ground flour.

"Bring your own containers, sisters, and form a line here. There is enough flour for each family to take four pounds."

"Do not worry, Annie." John squatted next to the campfire, practically inhaling Serena's leftover beans and Catherine's freshly baked biscuits. "President Olson told us more relief is on the way. The leaders from Great Salt Lake intentionally sent the first wagon of flour ahead of the rest, but several wagons of food and supplies are yet to come. We will survive, Annie. Thanks to Brigham Young and the Saints, we will survive."

"Good evening folks. It is a fine evening. Would you not agree?" I recognized Mads voice.

"Indeed, it is a very fine evening. Would you like to sit a spell?" Serena responded without hesitation. "Perhaps you would enjoy one of Catherine's biscuits?"

"Thanks for your generosity, Serena, but I came to speak with Annie."

Mads came frequently, in the evenings, when the winds had calmed and the camp quieted of cattle and noisy children. There were nights when Serena and I stayed by the fire, until only embers remained. There were other nights when Serena and the children left Mads and I alone, under the canopy of a million stars. We talked about our past, and our departed mates. We discussed our children, and our dreams for the future.

"Christine was a woman of faith. I have never known anyone that embraced the Gospel like she did. From the moment she believed, she began dreaming of Zion, and tried to convince me to also read the Book."

"Yes, and did you read it?"

"I tried to read, but it was difficult for me. I wanted to believe, but I was not sure. I did not want to disappoint her, and I feared if I did not agree to join the company going West, she would go without me."

Mads paused briefly before I began. "And now that she is gone, you are convinced it was all a mistake?"

"I have asked myself that same question a million times. Annie, I am not sure of what I think. I do know that Christine believed our children would be better off in Zion."

One thing I knew for certain, Mads was a lost, lonely man, still in love with Christine, the mother of his children.

I must admit the conversations with Mads were rather stimulating, and I enjoyed the growing friendship with Mads, but nagging thoughts took up residence in my head.

Jens and Mads knew each other. *What would Jens say of this man from Lihmskov? Would my children approve of a deepening relationship with Mads, perhaps a replacement for the father they adored? What of me? Could I even entertain the thought of being with someone other than Jens? Could I intentionally take on the responsibility of being stepmother to six additional children?*

"Moder, Moder!" Hans interrupted my pondering. "Duke is dead! Duke is dead."

"Oh, Hans. I have worried so much about our animals. I am so sorry."

John confirmed the devastating news. "After we watered the oxen, we were taking them to feed. Duke gave out a deep bellow, his legs buckled beneath him and without a warning, Duke died in his tracks. I am so sorry, Annie. Duke and Thunder have been so dependable, as leading yoke. Without Duke I am concerned as to how our remaining oxen will respond."

From the beginning, John had willingly assumed the responsibility of caring for our cattle and he had more than proved himself. John always made sure if water and grass was available, the four legged animals were fed. He had come to know each of the beasts, their stubborn personalities and how they each responded as a team. Losing Duke was not only a personal loss for John, but a devastating loss for our family. We dared not complain, however. We certainly were not the only family that had lost precious cattle and oxen. No one had to remind us that our progress, without the usual teams of oxen, would likely be slowed.

Way off in the distance we could see a dust cloud rising from what appeared to be a string of farm wagons, traveling east towards us. "That must be the wagons John told us about from the Utah Valley!" Hans shouted. "Moder, they are bringing us more food!"

Saturday, September 16th was a beautiful summer day with nary a cloud in the pale sky. The arrival of 16 farm wagons, pulled by mules, and loaded with relief, made the day even more glorious and memorable. "Brothers and sisters, we will be holding up in this camp for additional rest and recuperation. Be patient and we will get these wagons unloaded and the supplies distributed to you as soon as we are able." Brother Capson shouted.

The gifts of food not only brought the needed nourishment for the remainder of our journey, but the bags and barrels were wrapped with an emotional relief that was almost palpable. The near hopelessness of our company was lifted with a spirit of thanksgiving and celebration. Sunday morning we joined together in worship of the God we knew. Our voices filled the morning with joy and relief, and our prayers filled the heavens with praise and appreciation, for truly our prayers had been answered, and answered most abundantly.

Brother Christian Larsen preached a message from ancient scripture, a message filled with promise. "Scriptures tell us praise God in all things, and not allow fear to fill us with doubts of what shall lie ahead. Do not be distraught and think your trials are too hard. It is not so. All is right. For God is our guardian and guide, and if He should take us to our heavenly home before our journey's end, we shall rejoice, oh happy day.

"May you all find comfort in the promise from Nephi of old, 'And it came to pass that I, Nephi, said unto my father:

I will go and do the things which the Lord hath commanded, for I know that the Lord giveth no commandments unto the children of men save he prepare a way for them, that they may accomplish the thing which he commandeth them.' 1Nephi 3:7."

Our meetings ended with further instructions from President Olsen. "Beloved Saints, we will hold-up in this camp for an additional week. That will allow sufficient time to distribute the flour and supplies to every family. It will also allow the remaining cattle to rest and recuperate. Most of all, this week will give each of you time to heal and gain strength, enough to complete our journey."

"Margarethe, my dear friend, how good to see you. Please come sit with us." I sat with Serena around the few remaining embers of our campfire.

"Thanks, Annie. It is good to see you two women resting for a change!" Margarethe's teasing was just the sparkle that our conversation needed.

"Are you feeling rested and stronger, Serena? I am feeling quite lively since we received the additional supplies from Great Salt Lake, and have had time to rest." Margarethe explained.

"Yes, Margarethe. Both Annie and I are feeling much stronger. Please, sit right here." Serena motioned towards a small stool. "We have been talking about men and marriage. Perhaps you could give us another perspective! If Brother Lars, forgive me for saying so, was to die, do you think you would ever marry again?"

"Very interesting question, Serena. Brother Lars and I have been married longer than I care to remember, since I was very young. We have raised seven children and have had a wonderful life together. I can not imagine being with another man. No, I would not marry again! If something happened to Lars, I will go live with one of my children. Yes, that is it! Do not ever repeat what I just said, but I would just move in with Christian J. and his wife." Serena and I chuckled at Margarethe's confidence.

Serena rolled her eyes in disbelief. "You are very fortunate, Margarethe. I don't have a family member to rescue me, like you do. I had the very best husband anyone could imagine, but when he died I decided to remain single, at least until our children are grown. I am resourceful and have managed to feed my family so far. No, sisters, I don't think I would ever marry again. I certainly would never be a polygamist wife! Never!

"How about you, Annie?" Margarethe inquired. "I have heard a little talk about a certain gentleman calling on you in the evenings. Are you thinking about a future that might include Mads Powelson?"

My response was quick. "Oh, I see the gossip mill has been working overtime!" I hesitated briefly, smiled, and continued. "Margarethe, I do not have strong feelings either way. I believe, however, I must consider my children first. Hans and Yern have many years before they are grown, and they have so many things to learn, but most of those lessons can only be taught by a kind and caring man."

"Annie, if you are considering Mads, I can tell you. You will not find a better man. From the first time Brother Lars and I met Mads, he impressed us. He is one of the kindest, most patient fathers we have ever known."

"I appreciate your kind words, Margarethe. I will definitely take them into consideration."

Twenty-nine

$\mathcal{A}$ seven-day rest provided a much-needed respite for our company of weary worn-out emigrants. Rescue wagons, now carrying a number of our critically ill and elderly, turned around and headed for the Salt Lake Valley. One of the brethren, an experienced trail guide, stayed with us to provide further direction, especially for future camping sites.

No matter how hard I wished this journey could be over, I knew all the wishing and praying would not make it so. We had been well warned of the remaining miles of trail, and how the most difficult parts of the trail were yet ahead of us. Where could I find the physical and emotional strength to continue this journey? Filling my steps with prayer, I took my fears to the Heavenly Father I had come to trust. I plead in humility to the God that was my Father, to the God that cared for me even as the lilies, and to the God that had brought us to this barren land so far from civilization.

"Oh Heavenly Father, hear my prayers. I listened to the words of your missionaries and I believed. I left my homeland, trusting in faith, to follow your prophet. Surely you know how I have suffered, leaving my youngest son buried in Liverpool and another buried in the sea. I said goodbye to Jens, and left him buried along the Missouri River. Please, Oh Lord, help me find the strength to continue this journey. Do not forget me. Oh Heavenly Father, fill my spirit with a joyful song and fill my body with the strength that every step might feel lighter. Fill me with resolve, for I am weak, but Thy spirit can make me strong."

We followed along the Sweetwater, crossing the river at the seventh and eighth crossings into Sweetwater Canyon. The river cut through rock layers, making it impossible for the wagons to continue along the river's edge. The trail left the river, then stretched over continuous hills and ridges covered with dried sage. We climbed a gentle ridge between twin mounds, which formed a gateway to South Pass before we again camped by the Sweetwater. We would cross the river for the ninth and final crossing the next morning.

Mads sat near the fire, silently drawing circles in the sand with a willow. "When Christine and I met the missionaries, I was curious, but not as much as she seemed to be. She prayed with a great desire to know if the Book of Mormon was truly the inspired words from prophets of old. When she received an answer to her prayers, there was no one with greater conviction. Christine wanted to follow the prophets to America, but I did not want to leave our farm. Our farm was beautiful, and I had worked so hard to make it a place all my children would enjoy. I could not imagine selling my farm, and traveling to the far edges of this world, to a land unknown by civilization.

"Christine would not hear of my hesitation. She begged, she pleaded, and she prayed daily for a change of my mind.

I did, reluctantly. I sold our property, ultimately making Christine the happiest woman I ever knew. Now, without Christine, I am like a ship without the rudder. Annie, I do not know what I will do when we finally reach Zion. How can I claim a deed to land that is nothing but dried sagebrush, and start over again? Annie, I have six children to feed! Right now it all seems so impossible." The fire's light danced in Mads eyes as he tried to put words to his emotional loss.

I hesitated briefly, gathering all my courage to share my feelings without offending Mads. I wanted to share with him what I had come to know about faith, for it seemed to me that he was lost in his own pity. "Mads, I know what you are feeling. I think every person in this company has known the pain of losing someone they loved. In my own suffering, however, one thing I have come to understand. Our attitude will make the difference between an ordeal and an adventure."

I waited, letting my words take flight, and sink in. I was looking for some sign, any sign that Mads was understanding my implications. More than just a lesson for Mads, I realized my words were also a sermon for myself.

"We are in a time of testing, a time where the trail will sort the wheat from the chaff. The weak will be separated from the strong. Ultimately, our trials will make us stronger, if we have the proper attitude."

I continued. "Lift up your eyes, Mads, and muster every single ounce of faith you have. Fill your days with prayer and thanksgiving, and continue on, believing God will provide your every need."

Mads pushed himself to his feet, reached down and touched me on the shoulder. "Thanks for listening, Annie. I appreciate your honesty and words of encouragement." With that, Mads disappeared into the blackness of the night.

We trudged over high hills and through deep ravines. We climbed rugged canyons blocked by rock obstructions, crossing and re-crossing the willow-fringed Sweetwater. Now the oxen strained with all their might to pull the wagons up a barren incline known as Rocky Ridge. We followed behind, climbing and slipping over rugged boulders strewn across the roadway. We felt a new strength as we hurried past poisonous alkaline ponds, then Days Creek and Strawberry Creek, the highest point of the trail.

We trudged about eight miles across Aspen Ridge and on to South Pass. Brother Capson shouted as he rode alongside the wagons. "Brothers and sisters, we are now officially in Oregon territory. This is called the Continental Divide." The winds blew bitterly cold, but there on top of the world we beheld the beautiful snow-capped Windriver Mountains, forming an imposing wall on the western horizon.

From the South Pass our company paused briefly for water at Pacific Springs. We pressed on through the sand, sage, and thistles to the Parting of the Ways. Absent of any markers, our guides knew the trail. "Brothers and Sisters, listen up! You must keep your wagons on the left fork of the trail unless you want to end up in Oregon. The left fork will take us southwest into Utah territory and Zion."

We crossed the Little Sandy, a dried riverbed with nothing but sand, caked clay, sage, and thistles. "Brother's and Sisters, don't give up. Just a few more miles." Brother Capson encouraged us on. "We must get to the Big Sandy River before we camp. Our guide tells us we will find plenty of good water and grass for the cattle."

"Just a few more miles?" Catherine murmured aloud. "Moder, how can I possibly walk another step. Brother Capson must know that we are near exhaustion."

"Yes, I am sure he can tell how tired we are just by looking in our eyes. He knows."

"I do not know how he could possibly understand. He has been on a horse all the time!"

"Hush, Catherine. I am sure he would prefer being responsible for his own family, and not everyone else's."

The "moving on" was painfully slow, for everyone, including the oxen. We eventually reached the willow-banked river on September 18th. The surviving oxen, barely able to continue, pulled the wagons into the usual camp formation. There we found the oasis we had dreamed of; sweet grass for the cattle and pure clear water for drinking. We would remain in the Big Sandy camp for five days.

Even though the Big Sandy provided grass for the cattle, the relief was too late. After giving everything they had to give, our company suffered the loss of several more oxen. John and Hans struggled to save our own, but there was little they could do.

"Annie, we have lost Baldy. He was strong, and he pulled with every ounce of energy he could find, but in the end, he could not find enough strength to recover."

"Annie, come quickly. Klara is dying."

I could feel Klara's suffering as I knelt down in the tufts of grass beside my precious milk cow.

"Klara. I am so sorry. You gave your best, but we asked too much of you. We ask you to cross this desert, and on many days we could not provide enough food and water. I am so sorry."

The loss of Klara was a deep personal loss for me, for as long as Klara had milk, the two of us had spent the wee hours of every morning and the late hours of the evening together. I had relieved Klara's swollen glands while Klara listened to my frustrations, my doubts, and my most personal thoughts. "Klara, I will miss you." I wept.

"Annie, allow me." The voice behind me was that of my friend, Mads. Taking my hand, helping me to my feet, he brushed the tears off my face.

"I understand our leaders have organized a dance this evening. Would you honor me with your company?"

Brother Rasmus Olsen lifted his fiddle, nestled his chin into position, and bounced the bow over the strings, back and forth, providing an evening of welcome entertainment. His fingers flew over the strings as he pushed and pulled the bow, filling the night air with familiar music sounds from our homeland. The youngsters, filled with new excitement and energy, jumped up and down while the young adults danced and us old folks stood in the back, watching, helplessly tapping our toes, and clapping to the rhythm.

"Annie, dance with me!"

"Oh, Mads. Not here. Not now." I insisted.

"Come on, Annie, you will enjoy yourself."

Not to be deterred, Mads took hold of my hand. With some reluctance, I took his hand and we joined the youth, dancing around the circle, trying our best to keep in rhythm with the fiddle. Mads and I were the first of the old folks, but soon other couples joined the merrymaking. The night air was filled with hoots and hollers, singing and celebration. It was a grand evening.

"Thanks for dancing with me, Annie."

"You are quite welcome, Mads. I did enjoy myself. I felt young again, dancing like I did so many years ago."

"Annie, I have been thinking. We will be in the Great Salt Lake Valley in a few more days. We will be sent to stakeout our own homesteads, in uncivilized parts of the valley. We will be building new communities in the desert. I need a woman to help me. I need someone to help clear the land and to help care for my family. I admire your strength and your patience. I believe you are that woman. How can you possibly build a place for you and your children on your own? I want to be that man. I believe we will be successful if we become one family."

Mads waited for me to respond. I simply could not. I took a deep breath, hesitating. *Did I hear Mads correctly? This was a proposal of marriage? I didn't hear one word of affection, just words of 'need' and convenience.'* I searched but found no words, for they seemed to be stuck in a lump of hesitation and uncertainty.

Standing in awkward silence for what seemed far too long, I found the needed response to Mads' proposal. "Mads," I began. "I thank you for your kind words. I am honored that you think so highly of me. This is a decision that requires much consideration on my part, and for that reason, I must ask if you will be patient. Will you please give me time to consider your proposal?"

"Yes, Annie. Yes, I will wait for you."

Thirty

"Sixteen dollars for each wagon to cross the river?" I shouted. "Unbelievable! We do not have money to pay for a ferry. Will we be forced to cross the river on our own?"

"Annie. Wait." John motioned with his hand for me to hush. "The fees for the ferry are expensive, but we do not have much of a choice. Our scouts have examined every other possible crossing, but they say the Green River is too dangerous to cross without a ferry.

"However, we need not be concerned about the fees, Annie. Remember when we were in Westport, and our leaders ask for donations to purchase additional oxen? They purchased the oxen, but intentionally saved a portion of the donations specifically for ferry crossings. Every one of our wagons will be able to cross on the ferry and we will start in the morning."

Unlike the Sweetwater, which required us to cross and re-cross the water, we crossed the Green River but once. We camped for one week total; first on one side of the river, waiting for hours as each wagon and family was loaded on the ferry. One by one we crossed to the opposite side, to the "second" Green River camp. We prepared food for our families and we scrubbed our clothing, carefully draping each item over the willows to dry. We scrubbed our little ones in a small cove, where the willows provided the necessary privacy for bathing. Finally, with two sisters standing guard, lest some unsuspecting brethren should find us naked, it was our turn to bathe.

"The water is freezing!" I stuck one foot in the water and hesitated.

"Oh, Moder." Catherine was already in the water. "Moder, just get in the water. It is quite cold, but if you jump in, your body will adjust quicker than if you dawdle."

"Annie. We will only be in here long enough to get a layer of dust off our bodies." Serena's quivering voice confirmed the water was not to my liking. I hesitated, wrapping my arms around my nakedness while my friends chided and teased that I, too, should swallow my hesitation and join the chattering in the river. Reluctantly, I did.

"The first thing I am going to do when we reach Zion is to have a bath."

"I agree. When I get to Zion I want a warm bath, where I can sit and soak for an hour."

"It will take an hour to get all the grime off me!" Everyone laughed aloud.

"When I get to Zion I am going to find a room for bathing, a beautiful warm room with fragrant lavender water to caress my skin and beautiful linens to wrap around my body."

"Are you also going to have a maid to help you with your housework?"

Laughter erupted at the thought of such dreaming.

"Annie, forgive me, but I could not help seeing you walking with Mads. Please tell us, are you dreaming of lavender water and a warm bath in a house with Mads?" Karen's bold inquiry brought a sudden hush to the chattering.

I did not have a chance to answer. Serena answered for me, abruptly ending our late afternoon bathing. "Karen, I think your curiosity is perhaps more appropriately addressed somewhere other than in these frigid waters!" Serena stood up and walked towards the river's bank.

"I am sorry if I offended you, Annie. I should have held my tongue."

"No offense taken, Karen."

We dried our chilled bodies, wrapped our wet hair over our heads, covered our nakedness with layers of underclothes and finally a clean dress. The chattering and dreaming continued.

"When I get to Zion, I am going to have a new dress. A lovely wool dress with a ribbon at the neck and little buttons all the way down the front."

"When I get to Zion, I am going to have a house of my own, with glass windows, a hearth and handmade rugs on the floor."

Evening shadows were long before the wagons slowed to a halt and Brother Capson appeared, riding through our wagons, shouting out orders. "Pull your wagons into formation, brothers and sisters. We will be making camp here for the night. For your information, the small fort you see over there is Fort Bridger."

We learned Fort Bridger was not a military fort, but privately owned by the mountain man and trapper, Jim Bridger. The appearance of the buildings was small and ramshackle, but the site of the fort was opportune for Bridger because the paths of the Oregon Trail, the California Trail, and the Mormon Trail separated at this location.

"We are fortunate to have our people well stocked with supplies." Brother Capson continued. "A few of our men went over to the fort, and the prices of supplies would make a grown man weep."

Serena and I hung by the fire, hoping to get the needed energy to clean up the camp. Not a single spoon of beans nor crumb of biscuits remained in our pot, but the children were satisfied. "Have you seen Mads?" Serena inquired.

"Not since we left Green River. I think it unlikely that he will come to our camp this evening. Remember, I ask him for time to consider his proposal." I hesitated briefly, wondering if I should allow my thoughts to have words.

"Serena, I have thought about nothing else. For the last many miles, I have weighed out the advantages and disadvantages of Mads's proposal. I have been unable to reach a decision."

"I think Mads would be very kind to you, Annie. Take your time, however. This decision will not only affect your future, but the future of nine children!"

The night was long with frigid winds whistling through our tent. Our little family snuggled tightly, covered with every blanket we owned. Still, we nearly froze to death. I prayed that God would protect us from the bitter cold, and I prayed with all my heart for direction from above. *What am I to do, Lord? Should I marry Mads? You know, I don't love him, but Mads would help protect and provide for my children.*

In my sleeping, I thought I saw our Denmark farm, buried in a wintery blanket of snow. Candles flickered through the windows and sweet, spicy smells filled the air. Catherine and I were busy making pebernodder cookies, enough to share with our friends and neighbors. "Children, please! Sit down. It is time for Fader to read the Christmas story."

The children hushed, then gathered at Jens's feet, and waited for the deep familiar voice of their father to begin reading. "And it came to pass in those days, that there went out a decree from Caesar Augustus, that all the world should be taxed."

"Moder. Moder. Are you awake?" Hans whispered, gently touching my face. "Moder. I am going to start the fire."

Dazed from my slumber, and now quite awake, I realized it had been a dream. *Oh, how I missed the place I had called home. I missed the farm and our little family,. Most of all, I missed Jens. I loved him deeply. I only wish I had told him more often. Perhaps my dream had a particular meaning or a hidden message?*

Yes! That was it! I believed the dream was the answer to my prayers. I must never question myself again. Without a doubt, I knew what I should do.

Two days beyond Fort Bridger, the wagon trail descended the long steep canyon into Bear River Valley. The trail passed into a deep, narrow canyon known as Echo Canyon, with massive rocks rising up with astounding abruptness, soaring into the heavens. How insignificant we seemed next to the work of the Almighty's creation.

We trudged the trail along the banks of a good stream through fifteen miles of the wildest, most magnificent scenery, surpassing anything I had dreamed. We crossed and re-crossed the crooked stream that ran through the center of the canyon. Sandstone formations in colors of red, yellow and grey towered from 500 to 1500 feet above the valley floor and were given appropriate names like Rustic Cottage, Coyote Rock, Devils Post Office, Chicken-cock Rock, and Jack-in-the-Pulpit.

All the familiar creaking noises of our wagons, the lowing of cattle, or the braying of mules, were multiplied over and over as the sounds bounced down the rocks, echoing through the canyon, creating a noisy, interesting, romantic echo chamber.

Dwarfed by the surrounding Wasatch mountain peaks, we made what would be our last camp before climbing over Big Mountain and into the Great Salt Lake Valley. Nature's display surrounded us with groves of aspen, turned yellow and gold, a stark contrast against the dark green evergreens. The air, thin and crisp, rustled through the leaves, reminding us fall had indeed arrived.

The night was still young as we positioned the canvas tent and prepared our supper. "Do you children realize, this will likely be our last camp before we enter into the Salt Lake Valley?"

"Yes, Moder, we know. This valley is the topic of every conversation." Hans replied.

"What? You mean we will not be walking twenty miles a day for the rest of our lives?" Catherine winked and managed a smile.

"While our walking may be over, our working will have only begun!" Serena smiled politely.

"I wished I had stayed with my grandmother in Denmark." Ingeborg pouted. Her honesty was not surprising. This was not the first time we had heard similar complaints from our youngsters.

"John, I need to make sure you are planning to stay with us until you work off the debt for your passage, no matter where we are sent?"

"Yes, Annie. I am forever grateful to Jens for paying my passage. I will stay with you, under your employment, until I have repaid all I owe. Do not worry, Annie, I will be there to help you."

"Thank you, John. Having you to help us will ease much of the burden."

Standing tall, I looked into the eyes of our young ones and began. "I would like everyone to listen for a moment." I continued. "I am so grateful for every one of you. I have failed to tell you how proud I am of you. For that, I hope to change my ways. In the beginning, every member of our family was given particular responsibilities, and because each one has faithfully performed their work, we find ourselves within a few short miles of our destination.

"Know with certainty how much I love you. Catherine, Hans, and Yern, I want you to always remember that your father loved you. Ingeborg, Even, and Erastus, I know without a doubt, your father loved you. Each one of us are also loved and protected by our Heavenly Father.

"It was the desire of your parents to bring their families to the land of Zion, to the city high in the mountains, where we will find peace and prosper. Remember this my children and never forget, I have a sure knowledge of God, the giver of life and in His son Jesus Christ. We follow the teachings of ancient scripture, the Bible and the Book of Mormon, as well as the teachings of our modern-day prophet, Joseph Smith. It is my desire that you come to know this truth, as do I, and for generations to come, you will teach this truth to your children. Remember, oh remember what we have sacrificed for this truth."

Thirty-one

"*E*veryone! Look off there in the distance." Brother Capson pointed over miles of tree-covered terrain. "There is the Great Salt Lake Valley! The only obstacle remaining between us and the valley is Emigration Canyon!" There on the summit of Big Mountain, we caught our first glimpse of the valley below; the view, breathtaking, the remaining distance, daunting.

Our company of saints followed the narrow trail, hacked through densely wooded areas, winding along the valley floor and finally coming out on a natural land bench, overlooking the Great Salt Lake basin. I had painted this scene in my mind at least a hundred times, based only, of course, upon descriptions from the few who had actually been here. *This is the place? This is Zion?*

I strained to comprehend the distance, but as far as my eyes could see, north or south, lay a vast valley, sheltered by rows of mighty mountains on both the east and west. The sun cast warmth across the valley; a valley of nothing but a carpet of sagebrush. "Look over there, towards the north. Is that a cluster of buildings reflecting the sunlight?"

"Yes, Annie. You are indeed looking at Salt Lake City." John was filled with emotion, his voice quivering, "I can scarcely believe we are looking at Zion."

Standing high on a most perfect viewing space, inhaling

the magnificent valley, I was overcome with emotion. Tears filled my eyes, flooding down my dusty face and my knees felt weak, so much that I thought I might crumple to the ground. Here was the place of so many dreams, the place we longed to be, and with God's watchful care we had overcome the months of trials to now reach this paradise.

"Come, Moder. We have just a few miles to go." Catherine slipped her hand around mine, and together we walked the dusty dry trail. "Moder, I miss Papa so much and would give anything if he were with us now. He would be so proud of us for we have reached the place he longed to be. Zion! Moder, we have reached Zion!"

It was October 5, 1854, nearly one year since we had left our Danish home. Our wagons cast long shadows across the trail as a two-wheeled cart, drawn by a single ox, covered with a garland of wild flowers, led us into the city. We walked past roughly constructed log cabins and fine beautiful homes, some completed, and others under construction. We walked through the wide unpaved streets towards the center of a beautifully planned city. We trudged past gardens, filled with pumpkin vines and tomatoes, and homes lined with colorful marigolds and nasturtiums.

As the Salt Lake saints caught glimpse of our approaching wagons, they came from their gardens, houses, and places of business, shouting their greetings.

"Welcome to Salt Lake City."

"We are so glad you have arrived."

"Cheers for Zion! Welcome to Zion."

Many walked alongside us, briefly becoming a part of our company. Hundreds of people lined the streets, waving flags, clapping and cheering for our arrival. Union Square was already filled with people; wagons and cattle from an English company, having arrived just days before. Saints pushed through the crowd, looking for family members that might be in our company. "Do you know the Niels Borreson family?"

"Have you seen where the Christian Hansen family is camped?"

Thoughtful saints busied themselves passing out gifts of fresh vegetables and fruit. "Would you like an apple?"

"Please take this bag of potatoes." It was a grand, but chaotic reunion.

"Annie! Catherine! Gather the boys and come quickly." John shouted over the noise and confusion of the crowd. John pressed through the throng, our family tagging behind, to the edge of the square. There we beheld a mighty man in stature, shaking hands and greeting each one around him. "Annie, Catherine, Hans and Yern, this is Brigham Young. I knew you would want to meet him."

I hesitated. How could I shake the hand of this great man and leader? For that, I was not prepared. My hands were not clean. My clothes were dusty. Seemingly, that made no difference to the man who stood in the middle of the crowd, greeting everyone with great love and affection. He knew what we had been through because he had traveled that same tortuous trail just a handful of years before.

"Come, Annie. President Young wants to meet you." Stretching out my trembling hand, I shook the hand of Brigham Young. I shall forever remember that perfect day when I held, but briefly, the hand of a prophet of God.

"For those saints not having made prior arrangements for housing, Union Square will be our temporary home. We will camp here until we receive direction from Brigham Young as to where we will be sent." Brother Capson explained. "Meanwhile, I have exciting news for everyone. Our arrival in the Salt Lake Valley is perfectly timed with the Church's twenty-fourth semi-annual general conference. We will all be able to attend the three-day conference beginning in the morning."

John, understanding the English language better than anyone in our family, explained. "This ten-acre site was chosen for a temple by Brigham Young just days after he arrived. Brigham Young designed the temple to be the center of the city, with the blocks in a north, south, east and west grid from temple square. The fifteen-foot high adobe brick wall you see, that surrounds the temple area, was built to protect the construction which started last year."

Oh, what a glorious time we had. We gathered under an open-sided bowery, covered with branches, with thousands of faithful saints from the region and listened to God's word preached by authorities and leaders of the church. I understood but few words of English, however, it seemed to make no difference. Being there was enough, for I could scarcely contain my excitement. The meeting opened with a fiery, energetic hymn of praise. Thousands of harmonic voices filled the air and unexpectedly my body began quivering from head to toe. I was overcome by the spirit, hardly able to breathe. High in the mountains, in the center of a new city under the bowery of temple square I felt the spirit of Zion, and I chilled with the knowledge that God had spared us to see this day.

"Now I speak to our brothers and sisters of the Danish Company," Brigham Young's voice was loud and clear. "Welcome to Zion. I am pleased your arrival coincides with the beginning of our conference sessions, and I am exceedingly grateful to God for His mercy that brings you here today. For the purpose of building Zion, I am sending your company further south into an area where you can establish your farms and build your homes. A fort has been built on Cottonwood Creek and the beginnings of a new city wait for you. There is much work to be done, my brothers and sisters. Go forth, claim your land, plant your crops and build Zion."

"How far away is Cottonwood Creek?" Hans whispered.

"Shush..." I whispered. "I believe we will soon find out."

The days we spent in Salt Lake City were phenomenal. We feasted spiritually, praised God in songs, visited with friends, rested our bodies and emotionally prepared to move on. Brother Capson shared some of the details he had learned about Cottonwood Creek, the place we had been asked to settle.

"A fort has recently been built, and the settlement is known as Ephraim. We have been told Cottonwood Creek is about four days of travel, south of here. Only a handful of saints are living there, and they have built a fort for protection, should they need it, from a tribe of Indians also occupying the same area."

"Annie." Serena began. "Until now I have intentionally kept silent regarding my plans. I did so because I had not reached a decision about where I would go or what I would do, once we arrived in the valley. I must tell you after

President Young announced where we are to settle, I have prayed for guidance and I will not be going on to Cottonwood Creek. I have never had lofty intentions of staking out a land claim and building a home. How could I? I have no farm skills. I trust God will provide a home here in Salt Lake, where I can live with my little family, and a place where I can be employed."

How could I say goodbye to Serena? Until now I had not even considered the possibility of our company scattering. I found Serena's decision logical, but saying goodbye was like losing another family member, and I never was good at saying goodbye.

"I will miss you, Serena. You are an amazing, strong sister. I will miss the hours we spent talking about life's lessons, and I will miss the nights around our campfire. I learned much from you, Serena, but most of all you taught me courage and tenacity. I will be forever grateful to you. Please, we must not let distance keep us separated forever, and with heaven's help, we will find a way to see each other again."

"Thank you, Annie, for your kindness. I will miss you also but know this, my sister, you have more tenacity than you recognize."

"Serena, what of Karen or Margarethe? Do you know of their plans?"

"I am sorry, Annie. With all the crowds and confusion, I have not even seen Sister Neilsen or Sister Larsen since we came into the valley."

With John and Hans' help, we made our way around the wagons and cattle to find our friends that had become like family. One by one we shared of our individual plans. "Yes,

Annie, Brother Lars and I will be traveling with the company as far as Cottonwood Creek. We know nothing but farming, and it is our desire to build another farm for our children and grandchildren. Do not worry, Annie, we will be there to help you with anything you need." Margarethe put her assuring arm around me.

"Annie." Karen began. "Brother Nielsen is not strong enough to think of homesteading and farming, nor am I, so going to Cottonwood Creek does not sound logical for us. Jens has heard about a new settlement known as Lehi, south of here, about a days travel. We plan to stay with this wagon train until we reach that settlement, at which point we will say goodbye."

I understood. Embracing my friend from Bornholm, I bid her farewell. "Karen, you are a beautiful daughter of God, filled with more determination than I have ever seen. I am sure you will find the perfect place for a new home. God bless you and Brother Nielsen, and please, do not allow distance to make us strangers."

I had one more piece of unfinished business before our wagon train left Salt Lake. I had been avoiding the conversation I needed to have, far too long. "Hans, do you know where I might find Mads Powelson?"

"Yes, Moder, follow me, and I will show you where the Powelson family is camping."

I followed Hans, winding through the square, around wagons and people, rehearsing in my mind what I would say. *Be to the point, Annie. No need to explain in every detail the reasons for your decision. Be firm. Try not to be nervous.*

"Annie, so good to see you again. Hans, how are you, young man?" Mads stood, welcoming us into his camp. "I just heard Serena is planning to stay here in Salt Lake, and will not be going with the rest of us to Cottonwood Creek. Is that so?"

"Yes. It is true, Mads. Serena feels her chances of finding work will be much better where a community is already established. I am going to miss her terribly." I paused. "Mads, can we find a place to talk privately?"

Mads nodded, motioning for me to go ahead. "Hans, you know Mads's children. Please wait with them. I will return shortly."

I tried to gather my thoughts as we walked away from the commotion of camp. Mads made no attempt to rush me. "Many days ago," I paused, "you made a proposal of marriage, and I ask you for additional time to consider. I apologize for taking so long to respond, and for that I am sorry. I needed time to make certain my decision was the right one. After many prayers and much consideration, I must tell you my decision is to refuse your proposal.

"Please allow me to explain. Both you and I have lost our partners and only time can heal the loss. Your children are struggling over the loss of their mother, and they will resent anyone trying to replace Dorothea. Likewise, I believe my children will resent you because they love their own father."

Mads walked alongside me, quietly listening as I nervously continued. I was hoping to explain before Mads had a chance to interrupt. I took another deep breath. "John will be staying with me, at least until he works off the money Jens paid for his emigration. Hans has grown into a fine young man, and Yern is right behind him. Catherine is a beautiful, strong woman and she will be of great assistance. We have all talked together about our future, and we agree. We intend to stake out our own land claim and build the farm that Jens dreamed of. We can live in our wagon until spring, plant early wheat, and with the profits, we will be able to build a small home.

"Mads, I hope you understand." The walk back to where Hans waited was filled with awkward silence. I had said all I had hoped to say and I knew Mads would not try to change my mind.

"Hans, are you ready to go?" I slipped my hand into the sturdy arm of my eldest son and we maneuvered through the obstacles back to our wagon.

"Hans, you have grown into a fine young man, and I am so proud of you. How would you like to help John and I stake out a land claim and build a family farm? The first thing we need to do is find a piece of land to our liking near the creek. We will clear the land, by digging sagebrush, and picking up rocks. We will till the soil and plant winter wheat. We can live in the wagon for a short while until the brethren can help build us a home of our own. We will build our new home in tribute to your Fader, Hans. Are you ready to go stake out our land in Cotton Creek? Can I count on you to help build Zion?"

"Yes, Moder. You can depend on me. Let's go build Zion!"

SELECTED BIBLIOGRAPHY

Aird, Polly. Bound for Zion:The Ten-and Thirteen-pound Emigrating Companies 1853-54 -- http://files.lib.byu.edu/mormonmigration/articles/BoundForZion.pdf

https:/history.lds.org/overlandtravel/?lang=eng

http://www.utlm.org/onlinebooks/hothdiary_part1.htm

Heritage Gateways Pioneer 1838-1868 Companies http://heritage.uen.org/journals/

Jasperson, Hans autobiography

Jensen,Andrew. History of the Scandinavian Mission. New York: Arno Press, 1979

The Convert Immigrants -- http://history.lds.org/article/pioneer-story-the-convert-immigrants

http:/genealogy.pomosa.com/images/Lars%20Johansen%20Family/Johanson.txt

www.familysearch.org

www.findagrave.com

www.historytogo.utah.gov

www. independencerock.org

Pedersen, Lisbeth and Andreasen, Mads F. The Escape to America http://www.vestmuseum.dk/Viden/Midt-_og_vestsj%C3%A6llandsk_udvandring/AugustUK.aspx

Made in the USA
San Bernardino, CA
27 May 2019